A LOVELY LITTLE CHRISTMAS

A SHORT STORY COLLECTION

DEBBIE MUMFORD

WDM
Publishing

COPYRIGHT

PRAISE FOR DEBBIE MUMFORD

Praise for *Delectable Mountain Quilting*:
LW from Amazon: Five stars: *"Will read more of the series. Love quilting and related stuff. Story was gripping and well constructed."*

~

Jean from Amazon: Five stars: *"I enjoyed the easy read. A nice story with likable people. I used to quilt, so I understand the value of the antique quilt."*

~

Praise for *In a Pickle*:
Quilter from Amazon: Five stars: *"I'm a quilter and throughly enjoyed this story. I like a good series like this second book."*

~

Norrine B from Amazon: Five stars: *"Kept you on the edge of your seat. Good book for a snowy day in front of a fireplace with a warm beverage."*

~

Praise for *Second Sight*:
Bookgirl from Amazon: Five stars: "A lost love, a new love, psychic magic, a murder and a tiger! Wow. I loved this book. It was fast paced and easy to read. I got caught up in the "I'll just read one more chapter" syndrome and lost a bit of sleep but it

was worth it. I hope Ms. Mumford writes more in this world. I love these characters."

～

Dragon Slayer from Amazon: Five stars: "I liked the characters and the story line. For those that love a mystery and a good romance along with the paranormal, this book is for you."

～

Praise for *Sorcha's Heart*

Katie from Goodreads: Five stars: 'This story was fantastic...I strongly recommend anyone who likes paranormal dragon stories read this. Best prequel ever. Off to look for more by this author."

～

Old Ozark Gal from Amazon: Five stars: "...for those who enjoy a sizzling relationship without the graphic descriptions of what body part goes where, this is an excellent book. So what are you waiting for? Go read it!"

～

Karyn-Anne from Amazon: Five stars: "The romantic scenes were full of passion and heat, but not graphic or explicit. I really, really enjoyed this novella ... Very highly recommended!"

～

Ahmari from Amazon: Five stars: "This book is very well written ... I liked it so much I purchased the sequel! ... a unique idea for a fantasy and told in a delightful manner. I look forward to reading more from this author."

~

Praise for *Her Highland Laird:*

Katharina from Amazon: Five stars: "I'm normally not someone who reads romance novels, but ... I stumbled over Debbie Mumford's Romance stories. This one was an absolute treat. Not only did it depict the life in 15th century correctly (well researched for such a short story), it evokes emotion very well ... I'll definitely read more by this author."

~

Tony from Amazon: Five stars: "Very interesting story. With some suspense and an interesting thread of love."

DEBBIE MUMFORD

BESTSELLING AUTHOR OF SORCHA'S HEART

HER
HIGHLAND
YULE

A Logans of Lastalrig
Short Story

CHAPTER 1

Lady Catriona Logan swept into the great hall of Lastalrig Castle, her tartan skirt swishing around her ankles and her corsage laced so tightly she could feel her every breath. Hands fisted on hips, she paused to admire the decorations. The huge stone hearth at the far end of the room was swept clean, ready for the lighting of the Yule log when the men returned from procuring the traditional birch tree. The brass candle sconces fairly shone, having been polished for the festivities. Once the wicks were lit, the beeswax candles would cast a pearly glow on the rough stone walls. Fresh rushes were strewn across the flagstone floor, and the tables and walls were bedecked with holly, ivy, and mistletoe. In pride of place hung a beautifully woven kissing branch. The large spherical ornament was suspended from the rafters above a spot right in front of the head table where Cat and her highland laird Eideard would be seated.

Christmas at Lastalrig was like nothing Cat had ever experienced.

In the six months since she'd fallen through time to land in Eideard's life, she'd grown accustomed to the Scotland of 1452, but Christmas … well, Christmas was a time for family and friends, for beloved traditions like twinkling lights on a decorated tree, caroling in the snow, and lazy Christmas mornings with hot chocolate, cinnamon rolls, and beautifully wrapped presents under the tree.

At least, that was what every other Christmas of her life had been. But this wasn't 2012 and she wasn't in North Carolina with Gran Da. No, this year she was the Lady of Lastalrig Castle in the year of our Lord fourteen hundred and fifty-two. And it wasn't even Christmas they'd be celebrating tonight. It was Yule, and the festivities would last twelve days, with the biggest celebration occurring on Twelfth Night, January 5th, the Eve of Epiphany.

Eideard had explained it all to her, making sure she understood her role for the various saints' days that fell between Christmas and Epiphany, and she was somewhat familiar from her university studies of medieval literature, but reading about something that happened hundreds of years ago and experiencing it first hand were vastly different beasts. At least she knew she could rely on Eideard to guide her through the intricacies of the season.

Eideard. Her highland laird. The love of her life and the reason she was here, in a castle that was little more than a moldering ruin in the time she'd been born to. Eideard. He'd loved her enough to discover a way for her to choose her fate, and once she'd recognized his forbearance as love, she'd followed her heart and chosen to stay.

She smiled, remembering his declaration of love, "Ye are a trial, Catriona. How could ye doubt my love? Have I nae forborne tae beat ye when all my kinsmen hae counseled me that ye needed naught but a good lashing tae learn your place?"

A giggle escaped her lips and she glanced around to be sure she was still alone. She'd actually had to explain to the poor man that not beating her didn't equal love in a 21st century woman's mind!

But regardless of their vastly different communication styles, not to mention world views, Eideard did love Catriona, and Cat loved him so deeply, so completely, that she'd given up the opportunity to return to her own time, and instead worked daily to settle into her new life as the laird's wife, the Lady of Lastalrig.

And even though it was Yule, not Christmas, and gifts would not be exchanged for centuries yet to come, Cat would hold to her own traditions. Her hands relaxed from their fists and slid across the folds of her tartan skirt to rest protectively over the slight swell of her belly. Tonight, in the seclusion of their bedchamber, she would give Eideard the most precious gift she'd ever held: the knowledge that she carried his child.

CHAPTER 2

A few hours later, Cat sat beside Eideard at the high table enjoying a meal of roast goose and mince pies. The Yule log crackled merrily on the hearth providing both warmth and a rosy glow to the crowded room. Many of the members of Clan Logan had come to Lastalrig for the Yule celebration, and the castle teemed with life. Every room, except the bedchamber Cat shared with Eideard, boasted extra inhabitants, and the kitchens scurried to keep everyone fed.

Cat glanced at Eideard and her heart did a familiar little flip, raising her pulse. Her husband was easily the most handsome man in the room. Powerfully built with broad shoulders and a narrow waist, his dark auburn hair glistened in the firelight. He'd clubbed it at the back of his neck for the night's festivities, though Cat loved it best when it hung loose around his shoulders. As though feeling her gaze upon him, Eideard turned his head and smiled, his hazel eyes sparkling.

"Are ye enjoying the meal, love?" he asked, his English lilting with the Scots brogue she loved.

She nodded, heat suffusing her cheeks as she thought of how

his accent thickened when they made love in the private paradise of their marriage bed.

He grinned, and grabbing her hand, lifted it to his lips. "Ye are especially lovely tonight, Catriona. That new gown suits ye."

"Thank you, Eideard," she said, lowering her eyes demurely. "I'm glad my appearance pleases you."

Eideard chuckled, squeezed her hand, and, leaning close, whispered for her ear alone, "That was well said, my love. Ye'll have the clan believing ye are a well-bred lass yet." He kissed her cheek before continuing, "but 'tis a lucky man who knows the truth of who and what ye are … and that man is me."

Heat rose throughout her body, and she knew that her cheeks flamed to match the red of her new gown. She widened her eyes, met his gaze more boldly than any fifteenth century woman would dream of, and said with a very good imitation of innocence, "Why, my lord, I cannot imagine what you mean. I can assure you, my breeding is excellent."

Eideard guffawed. When his mirth had settled, he raised his goblet to her. "To yer health, wife."

Cat lifted her own cup and said with a smile, "And to yours as well, husband," and took a sip. Alone of all the revelers in the great hall, Catriona drank water. Boiled water. Though the castle's supply of drinking water came from a pristine spring, Cat had given Mistress Mac, the castle's headwoman, instructions that any water she and Eideard consumed was to be boiled first. As soon as she suspected her pregnancy, Cat had stopped drinking the ale that was served with every meal and insisted on water. Mistress Mac might think her strange, but the head-woman had long since accepted that the laird's wife held some distinctly odd notions.

After the remains of the meal had been whisked away to the kitchens, several of the clansmen pushed the large trestle tables away from the center of the room, clearing a wide area before the high table.

"What's happening, Eideard?" Cat asked, leaning close to her husband.

Eideard's eyes widened and his brows lifted in surprise. "Did ye no tell me that folk still carol in yer time?" he asked in a whisper.

"Well, yes," she said, watching in fascination as several pipers prepared their bagpipes, "but everyone could just as easily sit at table and sing. Why is so much open space needed?"

"Sit at table and sing? I can see we've verra different ideas of caroling," he said with a wry smile. "Watch and learn, wife. Clan Logan will show you what it is to carol."

With that, Eideard rose from the table and clapped his hands. The room quieted except for the residual hum of a pipe as it continued to bleed air. The laird left the table and strode to the center of the cleared space.

"As Laird o' Lastalrig, I claim the first carol. Who will join me?"

Cat watched in wonder as men and women rushed to the open area and formed a large circle around their laird. Those who didn't join the circle climbed onto the tables at the edges of the room and settled to watch. When all were in place, Eideard nodded to the pipers and began to sing in a rich baritone. The bagpipes caught his melody and the folk in the circle moved to the intricate rhythms of the carol.

The song was like nothing Cat had ever experienced. Eideard sang in Scots Gaelic, and while her grasp of the language had vastly improved over the last six months, she had trouble following the words, buried as they were in unexpected rhythms, the shuffle of dancing feet, and the screel of bagpipes. Cat sighed. If she'd expected to find comfort in the familiarity of *traditional* Christmas carols, she would obviously be sorely disappointed. Instead, she straightened in her seat and chose to enjoy the spectacle. Gran Da would never believe this!

When his carol finished, Eideard bowed to the dancers and

left the circle. Another singer took his place, a woman this time, and for a few moments the circle blurred as some left to sit on the tables and others took their places. Then, at a nod from the singer, the next carol began.

Eideard made his way back to Cat's side, dropped into his chair and drank deeply from his goblet. Wiping his mouth on his sleeve, he nodded to the circle. "That is how we carol at Lastalrig."

Cat smiled. "In my time, people walk about their neighborhoods in groups of five or six and sing Christmas carols. Or, if you're having a holiday party, everyone might sit around after dinner and sing. I've never seen carols accompanied by bagpipes and a circle dance."

Eideard shook his head, a small frown creasing his brow. "Everyone sings? How would they all agree on the melody?"

His words stunned her. "Agree on the melody? You mean it isn't standardized?"

He puzzled over her question for a moment before answering. "Standardized? Do ye mean everyone knows the carol? It doesna change with the singer?"

"That's right," she said with a nod. "The words and music are written down so everyone sings the carol the same way."

He stared at her. "How verra strange. Is it no boring to know exactly how it will sound?"

"Well, no. It's very comforting. You can relax into the music and remember other times, other places." Her eyes suddenly filled with tears as longing for her family and friends overwhelmed her.

Eideared picked up her hand and lifted it to his lips. "Dinna cry, lassie," he murmured. "Ye've home and family here now, and I'm verra glad ye chose to stay with me."

She wiped her eyes with her other hand and smiled at him. "So am I, my love." She drew a shuddering breath and turned to watch the carolers. "But it is so very different here."

When the next carol ended, Donal, Eideard's cousin and second in command, moved to stand before the high table. "Will the Lady o' Lastalrig not honor us wi' a carol?"

Cat's heart thundered so loudly that she almost missed Eideard's response when he rose to address the room. "My lady's customs are different," he said, his voice smooth as silk. "She is no accustomed to the dancing and the pipes."

She rose to stand beside him, squeezed his hand and said, "I'll gladly share one of my carols, and you're welcome to dance if you wish," she turned to the pipers and bowed her head, "but if you wouldn't mind, I'd ask you not to play."

The lead piper removed the blowstick from his mouth, bowed to her, and said, "We would be honored to listen to yer song, Lady."

Cat's thoughts raced. Which carol should she choose? Which would these people find most familiar? Which would make her seem least alien?

Eideard released her hand and seated himself beside her. The clan moved quietly out of the circle of dancers, waiting for her to begin.

When she sang the first note, the hall stilled. She hadn't realized she'd chosen until the words and melody emerged.

"Silent Night."

Her heart had chosen for her, and the choice was perfect. She sang the simple melody with all the warmth and longing in her soul. She sang for Gran Da and all the friends she would never see again. She sang for Eideard and the child growing within; for the future and the family they would build. She sang for Lastalrig Castle and the clan that had welcomed her, despite her odd ways. She sang for herself, for the woman she had been, and the one she was becoming.

When the last note faded away, Cat came to herself, suddenly embarrassed by the many eyes watching her. Then Donal began to clap and the hall filled with applause.

Eideard rose, pulled her into his arms, and whispered, "That was verra well done, Catriona. My people ... *your* people were moved."

When the hall quieted again, Donal bowed to her and said, "Thank you for sharing a carol, mi'lady." He turned to the hall and beckoned the people to gather. "Form a circle," he cried. "My own carol is burstin' to be sung!" And the hall filled again with what Cat was coming to recognize as Gaelic gaiety.

CHAPTER 3

The party, or *ceilidh* as Eideard called it, was still going strong a few hours later. The music had become more boisterous and the dancing more frenetic, but the energy in the hall remained cheerful and full of good spirits. Unfortunately, Cat's energy was flagging.

Though her pregnancy was still in the early stages, she tired more easily and found herself seeking solitude more frequently. Peace and quiet restored her soul, and this evening's feast and festivities had been anything but tranquil.

She turned away from Eideard and tried to stifle a yawn, but her husband was too aware of her to be fooled.

"Are ye tired, lass? Do ye wish to retire?"

She smiled wearily. "I'm fine," she said, another yawn spoiling her attempt to deflect his concern. "I don't want to spoil your fun. You stay. I can see myself to our chamber."

"Nay, my love. We'll go together. None in this hall would knowingly cause ye harm, but some men are too far in their cups to notice who ye are." He stood and offered her his hand. "Come."

She took his hand and stood, appreciating his steady strength as fatigue weighted her limbs. Together they left the hall, stopping here and there along the way to wish the joy of the season on various members of the clan.

When they reached their bedchamber, Cat sank into a chair before the hearth, blessing Mistress Mac for her foresight in seeing that the fire burned brightly.

Eideard knelt beside her chair and gazed earnestly into her eyes. "Are ye well, Catriona?" he asked, surprising her with his question.

"Of course," she said. "I'm just tired. It's been a long day."

He nodded, but his eyes continued to search her face. "Aye, it has, but ye seem to tire more easily these days. If there's aught amiss, ye'd tell me, would ye not?"

Her heart did a little backflip and she knew the moment had come. How she loved this man! She was out of her time and often out of her element, but he believed her, accepted her though she was so often not what the world expected of a woman in this time and place, and loved her wholeheartedly. The fates had blessed her when they had brought her to Eideard.

She smiled, joy flooding her soul. "Nothing is wrong, Eideard. In fact, something is very, very right." She took his hand and guided it to rest on her abdomen, the folds of her new red gown soft beneath their fingers. "I'm carrying your child," she said very softly, her voice husky with emotion.

Eideard's eyes had followed the movement of their hands, but now his gaze jumped to lock on hers and his hand spasmed on her belly.

"Truly?" he whispered. When she nodded, he asked, "Are ye certain?"

She laughed. "Well, if I were at home, I'd run down to the pharmacy and buy a pregnancy test, but since I can't pee on a stick here …" She stopped, seeing the bewilderment in his eyes. "Yes, Eideard," she said simply. "I'm sure."

He bounced to his feet, pulled her from the chair, and swung her into his arms. Holding her as easily as if she were a child, he spun in a circle before depositing her on the bed. "I'm to be a father!"

Landing beside her, he wrapped her in his arms and kissed her thoroughly. When they broke apart, he stroked her hair and asked, "When?"

"Uhm, given that I've never been pregnant before, I'm just guessing," she said, grinning at the impatient growl she both heard and felt. "But by my calculations, I think mid-July."

"Ye've made me verra happy, my love," he said, nuzzling her neck, "but ye are wearin' too many layers for me to properly appreciate the wonder o' the moment."

Later, as they lay spooned beneath the blankets, Eideard's hand splayed protectively across her belly, Cat spoke into the peaceful quiet. "You know, in my time, it's traditional to give presents at Christmas." She squirmed around in his arms until they were nose to nose. "I think this," she pressed his hand to her belly again, "is the best Christmas present either of us is ever likely to receive."

He kissed her tenderly, and then rested his forehead against hers. "I know 'tis one I'm no likely to forget."

She laughed and said, "I can't wait to meet this baby. I wonder if it will be a boy or a girl?"

He kissed her forehead lightly. "I dinna know, but whichever it is, I will love it until the day I die … just as I will its mother."

Lady Catriona Logan sighed happily, all nostalgia over Christmases past lost in the wonder of her first Highland Yule.

DEBBIE MUMFORD

BESTSELLING AUTHOR OF *SORCHA'S HEART*

Miss Bainbridge's
Christmas Party

CHAPTER 1

Miss Clarissa Bainbridge extended her white gloved hand to the footman and stepped into her father's well maintained black carriage. After tucking the woolen lap robe across her knees, she slid her gloved fingers into the depths of her white rabbit fur muff and sighed happily. Everything was in readiness for tonight's Christmas party. She had only to hand deliver one last invitation. Sir Gerald Lannington and his mother, Lady Helena, had only arrived in Albany yesterday evening, and this was Clarissa's first opportunity to issue their invitation. She did so hope they would be able to attend, despite the short notice.

After all, the party she had arranged would be the highlight of Albany's Christmas season. So many new trimmings in this Year of Our Lord 1830. Why gift-giving was now considered *de rigueur* and decorated fir trees were just coming into style, and Clarissa had ensured that her party was up to snuff in both areas! She and her mother and their maids had spent countless hours stringing popcorn and cranberries, making cut paper ornaments, and sewing small lace bags that would hold favors of hard candies and sugared nuts to be provided to each guest as a token gift as they gathered their great coats and pelisses to depart.

Everything was arranged to perfection, but the evening could only be enhanced by the presence of English nobility. It wasn't often that such refined personages deigned to spend Christmas in Albany, New York, and Clarissa was determined to add their glittering personalities to her party tonight.

She did so hope they would choose to attend!

Her carriage clattered to a halt on the cobblestone street, and Clarissa put aside the lap robe just as the footman opened the door. Allowing herself to be handed down, Clarissa gazed up at the stately townhome Sir Gerald and his mother had hired for their stay. The brownstone building rose two stories above a raised basement and boasted a small front lawn, now covered in a dusting of snow. A finely detailed cast iron fence and gate separated the yard from the street and a balustraded stoop rose to the main entrance.

Miss Clarissa Bainbridge lived in a townhome as well, but her family's dwelling was neither as broad nor as tall as this one, and her stoop was not nearly as grand as this fine example of Albany architecture. Of course, her family was not of noble blood, so allowances must be made.

Taking a deep breath, she nodded to the footman, who hurried to open the gate for her, and raising her skirts just enough to ensure good footing, mounted the stoop to the beautifully paneled and carved front door. Adjusting her pelisse and touching her fur trimmed bonnet to be sure it sat squarely upon her chestnut curls, Clarissa raised the iron door knocker and rapped twice. A few moments later, a liveried butler answered her knock.

"I am sorry, madam," he said, looking down his long nose at her, "but the family is not yet receiving callers. Would you care to leave your card?"

Clarissa inclined her head ever so slightly. "Thank you, Mister…" She paused waiting for him to supply his surname.

"Walters."

She smiled. "Thank you, Mr. Walters. Please see that her lady-ship receives this invitation and my card." Pulling the items from the lining of her muff, she handed them to Walters.

He glanced at her card, nodded, and said, "Very good, Miss Bainbridge. You may be assured that her ladyship will receive both at her earliest convenience.

Clarissa nodded and was turning to go when her foot slipped on an icy patch and she landed in a most undignified fashion on a hard brownstone step. Before she could do more than pull her pelisse and skirts more decorously around her legs both Walters and her own footman, Jenkins, were at her side.

"I say, Miss Clarissa," Jenkins said, kneeling beside her, "are you well?"

Walters sniffed. "Of course she is not well, you dolt. She's taken a serious tumble." He offered Clarissa his hand. "Do you think you can stand, Miss?"

Clarissa accepted the proffered hand and made a brave attempt to rise. Pain shot from her ankle all the way to her heart the moment her foot touched stone. She cried out and collapsed again to the cold, hard surface of the stoop's top step.

Walters knelt beside her. "If I may presume, Miss, I'll carry you into the parlor and call one of the maids to assist you."

Jenkins planted his fists on his hips and glared at Walters. "Here now! If anyone is to take liberties with Miss Clarissa's person, it shall be me." He turned his gaze on the young lady. "Come now, Miss. I'm sure you'd rather I bundled you into the carriage and saw you home, wouldn't you?"

Clarissa grimaced. "Thank you, Jenkins, but I don't think I could endure the swaying and bumping of a carriage ride right now. Mr. Walters, you have my permission to attempt to lift me. If I am too much for you, I'm sure Jenkins will assist."

"Not to worry, Miss," Walters said. "A little slip of a thing like you won't be a problem." And placing one arm behind her back and the other beneath her knees, the butler lifted her carefully from the step and carried her through that lovely front door and into the parlor, Jenkins following close behind.

When she was settled on a sofa with her injured foot propped on a pillow, Walters rang for a maid. While he was explaining that the young lady had taken a fall and would need assistance removing her pelisse and fur hat, Clarissa turned her attention to Jenkins.

"If you would be so kind, Jenkins, please return home and inform Mother what has happened. Tell her that I've likely sprained my ankle, but that I should be home well in advance of the Christmas party."

Jenkins bowed. "Of course, Miss. Shall I come back to collect you?"

Walters, overhearing this remark, said, "That won't be necessary, young man. When Miss Bainbridge is ready to leave I shall order her ladyship's coach to convey her."

Clarissa nodded her thanks.

"Now, if you'll be good enough to make a detour and deliver a note to her ladyship's physician, I think we should retire and allow Ellen to help Miss Bainbridge out of her pelisse." So saying, Walters ushered Jenkins from the room and pulled the parlor's sliding doors closed.

CHAPTER 2

Miss Clarissa Bainbridge rested at her ease on the thickly cushioned sofa in the front parlor of Lady Helena Lannington's Albany residence. Her ladyship's maid, Ellen, had taken Clarissa's pelisse and hat, smoothed her chestnut curls, and provided her with a cup of hot tea, sweetened with milk and sugar, and a plate of shortbread cookies, though Ellen had referred to them as *biscuits*.

Now Clarissa awaited the arrival of the physician, whom Walters assured her would come immediately on receipt of the note written on her ladyship's stationary. While she waited, Clarissa took note of her surroundings. While she understood that the Lanningtons had hired the brownstone furnished, she was nonetheless fascinated by the graciousness of the room. The walls were painted a pale, new-leaf green, with the woodwork a very slightly darker shade. The central area of the hardwood floor was covered in a Turkish carpet of tasteful design. Sheer lace glass curtains covered the two windows, their heavy, brocade drapes of deep forest green were tied back allowing light into the room. Matching brocade valances completed the window treatment.

The furnishings were classic and elegant. The sofa— upon which Clarissa now reclined, loveseat, and several arm chairs were upholstered in a vine and rose patterned damask, as were several ottomans. The circular tea-table, lamp tables, and sofa tables were of cherry wood and polished to a high sheen, as was the elaborately carved curio cabinet in the corner. The fireplace, with its merrily dancing flames, was as ornately decorated as the rest of the furnishings, and the intricately designed iron fire screen was a thing of beauty.

Clarissa had just finished cataloguing the room's decorations when she heard voices in the hall. Perhaps the physician had arrived? She hadn't heard a knock or the opening of the front door, but her mind had been rather occupied with memorizing the furnishings in order to share the details with her mother at a later time.

Footsteps sounded on the hardwood floors of the hall and then the parlor doors slid open. Walters stepped into the room, his back ramrod straight. He cleared his throat to assure her attention, and announced, "Sir Gerald Lannington."

The gentleman who entered the room wore a dark gray morning coat, matching waistcoat, white shirt, and dove-gray trousers. His dark hair was side-parted and he sported mutton chop whiskers. Clarissa knew Sir Gerald to be of marriageable age, but had not expected the man to cut quite such a dashing figure.

"Sir Gerald," Walters continued, "Miss Clarissa Bainbridge."

"Please forgive me for not rising, sir." Clarissa's cheeks heated at her inability to stand and offer Sir Gerald the required curtsy.

"Not at all, Miss Bainbridge." Sir Gerald's voice was a very pleasing baritone, and Clarissa watched through her lashes as he strode into the room to stand near the fireplace. "I'm only sorry that our stoop has caused you injury." He glanced at Walters, who remained near the parlor door. "Has the physician been summoned?"

"He has, sir."

Sire Gerald nodded. "Very well. You may go, Walters. Please have Ellen inform Mother of our guest."

"At once, sir." Walters departed, leaving the parlor door open, as was proper in mixed company.

Sir Gerald turned his attention to Clarissa. "If I may ask, Miss Bainbridge, what brought you to our door this morning?"

"Oh! In all the commotion, I quite forgot." Clarissa clasped her hands in her lap and glanced toward the open door, wishing Walters would return. "I brought an invitation for you and her ladyship to a Christmas party this evening. I'm afraid I gave it to Mr. Walters prior to my... uhm... my fall."

"I see. No doubt Walters has sent it up to Mother." He waved the matter away, but then glanced at Clarissa again. "I doubt we'll be able to attend. It *is* rather short notice."

"Of course," she said, "though you did only just arrive in town and I didn't want to offend by failing to issue the invitation."

His eyebrows winged up and he cocked his head. "I'm sure neither Mother nor myself would have taken offense, but it was very good of you to extend the courtesy."

He smiled as he uttered these words, and Clarissa wished for a fan. Not only did she need to cool her heated cheeks, but she would have appreciated the ability to hide her face... and perhaps peer at him from behind the safety of the fan's screen. Lord! She'd found the man dashing before, but when he smiled! Well, Sir Gerald Lannington was quite the most handsome man she'd ever seen.

CHAPTER 3

Sir Gerald Lannington observed the young lady currently resting on his sofa, considered the actions that had placed her there, and decided she was quite the most interesting person he'd encountered since arriving upon American soil. He and his mother had spent a month in New York City and had received numerous invitations to dinner parties, theatrical evenings, and even a ball or two, but none of the hostesses of those events would have dreamed of hand-delivering the invitation. That was what servants were for, after all.

And yet this pretty young female had made the effort to present herself at his door just to ensure that he and his lady mother would know that their arrival had been noted and that their attendance at tonight's party was desired. She'd undoubtedly assumed they would not attend. Not on such short notice.

And yet, the effort had been made… and an injury sustained.

Remarkable.

Uncertain of his next conversational gambit, Sir Gerald was about to withdraw to the window when he heard the unmistakable sound of his mother's footsteps. Two beats of her fashionable leather boots accompanied by the thump of her cane and the swish of heavy silk skirts. He crossed the room to the open door in time to usher his mother inside, waving Walters away as he did so. No need for a second formal announcement.

Taking his mother's free arm, he led her to an upholstered arm chair. When she was comfortably settled, he took his own seat and made the introductions.

"Mother, this is Miss Bainbridge." He nodded to Clarissa. "Miss Bainbridge, my mother, Lady Helena Lannington."

He noted with pleasure— odd, really. Why should the young lady's good manners please him?— that Miss Bainbridge refrained from speaking until Lady Helena opened the conversation.

"I'm told you took a fall on our front stoop, Miss Bainbridge. Are you quite comfortable?"

Clarissa inclined her head and lowered her eyes as she replied. "Yes, my lady. Walters and Ellen have taken pains to see to my comfort." She bit her lip lightly before continuing. "I must apologize. I had no thought to intrude upon your privacy and will be gone as soon as the physician has pronounced me fit to travel home."

While the two ladies spoke of trivialities, the weather and the dangers of icy steps, Sir Gerald studied the pair of them. His mother, a striking dowager with meticulously coiffed gray hair under a lace cap, and the lovely, petite Miss Bainbridge. The young lady's chestnut hair was modestly styled with ringlets falling to the shoulders of her pale blue morning gown. A stray lock had escaped, forming a small curl at her temple. He found that little curl absurdly charming.

"Don't you agree, Gerald?"

Sir Gerald startled. Yanking his thoughts from the contemplation of Miss Bainbridge's curls, and perhaps even the imagined softness of her lips, he said, "What? I'm sorry, Mother, I'm afraid I was woolgathering."

"Honestly, boy," Lady Helena huffed. "Do try to pay attention when we are in company. I said, we are much too fatigued by travel to attend a Christmas party tonight. Do you not agree?"

Sir Gerald glanced at Miss Bainbridge, who had bitten her lower lip and fluttered her lashes in quite the most adorable fashion when his mother had rebuked him, and saw disappointment bloom in her lovely blue eyes. A sudden wish to please overcame him. He simply couldn't allow her to be disappointed. Not if it was within his power to prevent.

He turned to his mother. "If you are overtired, Mother, then of course you must remain in residence for the evening." He smiled at Miss Bainbridge. "But I would not miss this party for the world."

CHAPTER 4

Miss Clarissa Bainbridge sat enthroned like a princess in a wing backed chair beside the Christmas tree. Her injured ankle rested on a cushioned footstool, and though she fidgeted, wishing she could see to the myriad last minute details before the guests began arriving at her door, she kept her seat. After all, Lady Helena's physician had been very firm. She would only be allowed to return home, where a grand party was scheduled for that evening, if she promised to stay off her feet. She was not to put weight on that ankle for at least the next several days.

She had given her word.

Of course she had given her word! Had not the very handsome Sir Gerald Lannington agreed to attend her Christmas party? How could she possibly miss what was now certain to be the event of the season? Even if missing said event would mean she was forced to remain in the Lannington household?

She would far rather attend the party, even if she did have to remain seated, than to spend the evening tucked up in an unfamiliar bedchamber.

Besides, Sir Gerald could hardly visit her in her bedroom, but she had hopes that he would condescend to converse with her for at least a few moments during the party.

So she sat as quietly as she could manage while her mother and their maids, Darcy and Emma, lit the candles on the tree. When her father joined them and laid a hand on her shoulder, she breathed out a happy sigh.

"It's a lovely sight," her mother said, pinching out her taper, and stepping to join her husband and daughter.

"I must admit, I had doubts about bringing a tree into the house," Clarissa's father admitted, "but it does make a pretty sight."

Clarissa clapped her hands, joy filling her heart. "It's absolutely magical."

Just then Jenkins, who was performing the role of under butler for the party, ushered in the first guests. As her mother and father moved to welcome the new arrivals, Clarissa studied the Christmas tree. Cranberries and popcorn. Cut paper and candles. A small, well-shaped fir tree. Who would have thought such simple ingredients could combine to create such a beautiful vision?

She was delighted that her family had been among the first to adopt what had seemed a somewhat outlandish idea, and now that she had seen it arrayed in all its finery, she was determined to make it a Christmas tradition.

"Your tree is quite the loveliest I have yet seen."

Startled, Clarissa turned her attention from the tree to find Sir Gerald standing beside her chair.

"Oh! Sir Gerald," she said, once again wishing for a fan to hide behind. She knew he was to attend, knew he had this effect on her. Why, oh why hadn't she thought to have Emma fetch her white lace fan?

Of course, she knew why the fan had been overlooked. Dressing in her best ruby red silk dress with white lace accent at bodice and cuffs had been difficult to manage while avoiding placing any weight on her injured ankle. Emma had had quite enough to deal with without intuiting that her mistress would be in need of a fan to hide behind during the party.

Clarissa lowered her eyes and hoped any pinkness in her cheeks would be attributed to the candlelit tree and the excitement of the party in general, rather than the nearness of the estimable Sir Gerald.

"I didn't realize you had arrived."

"I only just walked in," he said. Was that a twinkle in his eye, or simply a reflection from the candles on the tree? "You made such a pretty picture sitting here beside the tree that I had to give you my compliments."

Clarissa's heart leapt and she knew her cheeks must be flaming, but she couldn't deny his words pleased her beyond reason.

Glancing around the room, he gestured to a straight backed chair with a needlepoint cushion, and asked, "Might I be permitted to rearrange the furniture and join you?"

Clarissa's mouth went dry and her tongue felt glued in place, but she managed to whisper, "Of course."

A warm glow settled over her person as Clarissa watched the handsome young Englishman stride across the room. The very same young man who had seen her home after her morning's adventure. Who had insisted on carrying her inside— against her protests that it was unseemly, that Jenkins could unquestionably accomplish that task in his stead. The young man who had convinced his lady mother to attend the party this evening, and who was even now preparing to do her the singular honor of sitting beside her and keeping her company during the party, the gaiety of which now swirled around her.

As Sir Gerald hefted the chair and prepared to return, Lady Helena appeared at Clarissa's side.

"I do believe my son is smitten, young lady," the dowager said, thumping her cane to assure Clarissa's attention.

Clarissa quelled her nerves and turned a wide-eyed gaze upon the older woman. "Oh, Lady Helena! I'm sure you are mistaken."

"I most certainly am not." Lady Helena tilted her head and studied the young lady ensconced in the wing-backed chair. With an almost imperceptible nod, she continued, "I know my son, and his every mood." She patted Clarissa's arm and smiled. "Be careful of his heart, my dear, for it is the greatest Christmas gift you will ever receive." And stepping away, she made room for her son to place a chair beside the very pretty, and now visibly flustered, young lady.

And that is how a slip on an icy Albany stoop caused Miss Clarissa Bainbridge's Christmas party to become her final such seasonal event... for the next year she was no longer Miss Bainbridge, but Lady Clarissa Lannington.

Christmas Star

A Short Kristi Lundrigan Mystery

DEBBIE MUMFORD

CHAPTER 1

Kristi Lundrigan sat comfortably curled into the corner of her leather sofa, a king-size quilt covering her lap and a good portion of the sofa, while fat snowflakes drifted lazily outside the window. Her television was tuned to a cable station that featured a yule log blazing in a river rock hearth with traditional Christmas carols playing in the background. A cozy setting to finish the work she'd started over a month ago.

Kristi loved to create quilts and had converted one of her Garnet Gateway, Montana home's three bedrooms into a well-designed studio, but this final stage didn't require her state-of-the-art Viking sewing machine. Kristi much preferred to hand stitch the quilt binding in place, and hand stitching could be done in comfort of her living room where she could enjoy her Christmas tree, the yule log video, and listen to carols wafting through the room.

Stitches and Between, Kristi's moggy cats, also approved of her change of venue. Stitches, her gray tabby female, rested on the back of the sofa near Kristi's shoulder, while Between, her little tuxedo male who'd been named because his claws reminded Kristi of the tiny, sharp needles used in hand quilting, curled on the hassock where Kristi had been resting her feet until a few minutes ago. Both cats purred contentedly, pleased to have their human in their domain.

"Not long now, kitty-kids," she said, smiling at her feline companions. "When I finish this seam, we'll lay this Christmas Star quilt out on the bed, snap a picture or two, then call Mark and ask when I should deliver it." She smiled in satisfaction.

The quilt had been a delight to make. Mark Robards, her friend and the contractor who had remodeled her quilt shop, *Delectable Mountain Quilting*, had commissioned the quilt in early November after asking if she could have it ready before Christmas. The man had been firm on the pattern, only a Christmas Star quilt would do, and had even come into Kristi's shop to help choose the fabrics. The background was a lovely tone-on-tone muslin, while the stars shone brightly in red and green quilting cottons. Very Christmassy.

Kristi was curious as to why Mark wanted a king-size quilt for Christmas, but since he'd only smiled when she'd asked the question, she'd refrained from asking again. And to add to the mystery, he'd cautioned her not to mention the quilt when she saw him around town. If she had questions, she should call him. Very secretive.

After taking the final stitches and tying off her thread, Kristi gathered the quilt in her arms and strode to her guest bedroom. The quilt was too big for the queen size guest bed, but it made a pretty picture nonetheless. She was pleased with her work and hoped Mark would be too.

"All right, kids," she said to the cats who had followed her into the usually closed off room and were patrolling its edges and sniffing the corners. "Time to deliver Mark's quilt."

CHAPTER 2

The next afternoon, Kristi met Mark at *Roasted Beans* to hand off the quilt. The popular coffee shop sat on a busy Main Street corner and was a favorite haunt for most of Kristi's friends. She'd hoped Mark would come into her shop to pick up the quilt so she could spread it out in the classroom and see Mark's reaction to her work, but he'd declined. He didn't want her employees to know about the quilt.

To say she was disappointed was an understatement. If there was one thing quilters loved, it was showing off their finished quilts to an appreciative audience, and Kristi was no exception. As every quilter knew, there was no better audience than quilt shop employees and their customers!

Bummer. She wouldn't get to see Mark's reaction and she'd miss the opportunity to bask in the praise of her customers and coworkers over her accomplishment.

Oh well, this was Mark's gift, not hers. She'd just have to settle for the monetary reward… and the satisfaction of a job well done.

Mark sat at one of the little glass-topped tables that lined the coffee shop's window walls sipping from a white ceramic mug.

Kristi smiled, knowing his preference for unadulterated black coffee. When he glanced up, she waved and moved to join him at the two-top table.

He stood as she approached. "Don't bother ordering," he said with a smile. "The barista will be delivering a chai latte momentarily."

She laughed. "You know me too well!"

He nodded to the large paper bag she carried by its handles as they slid into their seats. "Is that what I think it is?"

"It is indeed," she said, grinning. "I can hardly wait to hear how you like it."

Conversation ceased as a pretty young woman approached their table carrying a steaming white mug. Kristi thanked her, then closed her eyes and inhaled, enjoying the aroma of the creamy goodness contained in the mug. Black tea subtly spiced, fragrant with cinnamon, black pepper, and ginger, and just the right amount of sweetness. After a moment, she took a careful sip of the hot liquid, savoring the rich blend of flavors that exploded on her tongue.

Mark ignored his coffee as he frowned down at the paper bag now sitting on the tiled floor beneath the table. "It really fits in that bag?"

"Yep. I've folded it carefully, placed it in a king-size pillow case—warn whoever you give it to never to store it in plastic—and stuffed it into that bag. No one will see it until you decide they should." She took another sip of chai, placed her mug on the table, and continued. "Also, if you, or whoever, are going to store it for long periods, be sure to refold it periodically so that the fold lines don't damage the fabric."

He nodded. "Right. I'll have... the recipient... contact you after Christmas for instructions about the care and feeding of," he leaned toward her and lowered his voice to a barely breathed whisper, "quilts."

Her eyes widened at his unwillingness to even say the word in a normal voice. Mark took his secrecy seriously. What was the man planning to do with this quilt? She sincerely hoped she'd find out eventually.

Pulling an envelope from his jacket pocket, Mark handed it to Kristi. "Here you go. As agreed, with a little bonus for delivering it well in advance of Christmas Eve."

"Oh! That wasn't necessary, Mark," she said, accepting the envelope. "But extra cash is always welcome, especially at this time of year. And I do still have a bit of Christmas shopping to do."

Leaning back in his chair, Mark folded his arms across his chest a satisfied expression on his face. "I can't tell you how grateful I am that you finished it in time... and three days early to boot!"

Kristi laughed. "Me too. What say we celebrate tonight? Call Stacy and see if she'd like to have dinner at *Rizzoli's*. Jason won't be a problem. He and I have a standing dinner date."

Mark frowned. "Sure, but we can't say..."

"I know, I know," Kristi interrupted. "There'll be no mention of what we're celebrating, other than the season."

Mark's expression cleared. "Perfect. You corral Jason and I'll round up Stacy. Does eight work for you?"

Kristi nodded, finished her chai latte, and prepared to leave. "It's a date. See you tonight."

CHAPTER 3

Kristi had just finished putting the finishing touches on her make-up when a knock sounded at the front door. She smiled. That would be Jason, her ex-husband and current love interest was always prompt. After their divorce well over a year ago she'd never have believed that they could even be friends, and yet, here they were, dating again.

Jason Reynolds was not only the sheriff of Garnet County, Montana, he was also her personal hero. He'd saved her life when a murdering mad woman had decided Kristi had to die… and that close call with death had opened both their eyes. They might be divorced, but there was still a lot of love between them. They'd decided to try again, but were taking things slow and easy as they worked to rebuild the trust his infidelity had destroyed. They'd come a long way in the eight months since that harrowing event.

Opening the front door, Kristi drank in the sight of the only man she'd ever loved. Tall, well-built, with wavy chestnut hair and steely gray eyes that were currently almost blue as he studied her with obvious appreciation.

She'd dressed carefully for their dinner celebration in a festive red velvet dress with deep green trim at neckline and cuffs. She and Mark might be the only ones who knew exactly what they were celebrating, but that was no reason to miss the opportunity to dress up. She'd styled her shoulder-length blonde hair in a sleek French roll, leaving a loosely curled strand on either side of her face, and highlighted her blue eyes with a subtle application of eye shadow.

Pulling herself out of her appreciation of the man, she smiled and opened the door even wider. "Would you like to come in for a minute, or are we in a hurry?"

He grinned and stepped past her into the warmth of her living room. "I think we have a few minutes." He removed his dark gray Stetson as he reached for her hand. "You look amazing, Kristi. Even more so than usual."

Her cheeks heated in a blush. The curse of fair skin! "You clean up nicely yourself."

And he did. Usually when they met for dinner, he was still in his sheriff's uniform, complete with holster, gun, and badge. Tonight he wore a western suit in dark charcoal gray with a light blue shirt and string tie. In a nod to Montana's December weather, he'd topped the suit off with a black leather duster.

As he settled on the couch, he glanced around the room. "Your tree looks nice." He paused to lean forward and greet Between, scratching behind the little male's ears. "I haven't bothered to put one up," he said, glancing from the cat to Kristi. "I'm rarely home long enough to enjoy it."

Kristi nodded, settling into an overstuffed chair across from him. "I understand the feeling. We decorated the shop, and for a little while I considered leaving it at that. But I wasn't ready to leave all my ornaments in a box, so the kitty-kids and I put up a tree."

Jason's eyebrows rose. "And how are the cats doing with the tree? Have they broken anything yet?"

She laughed. "Actually, they've been really good. I let them explore the boxes and showed them a bunch of the ornaments before placing them on the tree. That seems to have satisfied their curiosity." She paused as Stitches ambled into the room and settled on the tree skirt. "That, and I gave them each a soft ornament filled with catnip."

"Aha! You bribed them!" His eyes crinkled with delight.

"Yep. And so far, it's working." She glanced at the clock on the mantle. "Would you like a beer or anything, or should we get going?"

Jason slapped his knees and gathered up his gear. "Let's head out. We don't want to keep Mark and Stacy waiting."

When they stepped into *Rizzoli's Fine Italian Restaurant* Mark waved them over to a four-top table covered in a red and white checked tablecloth and sporting a raffia covered wine bottle candleholder decked out with a red ribbon and a sprig of holly. Stacy Akins sat beside him, wearing a red plaid dress with festive gold and silver clips in her dark brown hair. Stacy had been the realtor who sold the quilt shop to Kristi. She'd also recommended Mark for the remodel work. They hadn't been dating at the time, but by the time Kristi recovered from her nearly fatal encounter with the murderer, they'd become an established couple.

The foursome greeted each other, exchanging compliments all around, then settled into the serious business of deciding what to order. The scents of oregano, thyme, and garlic, as well as frying meat and just a hint of melting beeswax surrounded Kristi with comfort, while the gaily decorated tree in the corner and swags of pine over the windows provided just the right seasonal touch.

After ordering, the four friends chatted amiably, bringing each other up to date on their lives. Kristi, of course, neglected to mention the quilt that had occupied so much of her time recently. Mark gave her a conspiratorial wink at one point, but neither Jason nor Stacy appeared to notice.

When their food arrived, all conversation ceased as they dug into their meals with the gusto the rich Italian food deserved. Kristi had ordered her favorite, a steaming plate of flavorful lasagna and a generous tossed salad. She scooped up a bite of perfectly spiced beef, rich tomato sauce, and generous layers of gooey cheese and perfectly cooked pasta and closed her eyes, the better to savor the flavors. The bottle of Chianti wine Mark had ordered complimented the meal perfectly. The red wine's tart cherry flavor, along with its alcohol content, made Kristi want to purr with satisfaction.

Mark and Jason were busy devouring huge servings of spaghetti and meatballs, while Stacy worked delicately at a plate of fettuccine alfredo. When their meals had been decimated and the wine enjoyed fully, Mark pushed his plate away and leaned back in his chair.

"Who's ready for dessert?" he asked.

Stacy turned to him, her eyes huge. "You've got to be kidding! I couldn't eat another bite."

"Me neither," Kristi agreed.

Jason glanced from Stacy to Kristi, then grinned at Mark. "If that's a challenge, I'll take you on," he paused when Kristi gasped, "but otherwise, I'm content to pass."

Mark laughed and reached across the table to bump knuckles with Jason. "We're nothing if not competitive. Okay. No dessert tonight, but sometime during the holidays we have to get together for yule log cake or fudge or even Christmas cookies."

"That sounds great," Kristi said enthusiastically.

"I know!" Stacy said. "Let's get together on Christmas Eve!"

Mark's eyes widened and a look of panic crossed his face.

"None of us has extended family here locally," Stacy continued, seemingly unaware of Mark's reaction. "So we can be our own little family. What do you say? Come over to my house on Christmas Eve and bring your favorite dessert. I'll set out a simple buffet, maybe a fondue or something."

Kristi glanced at Jason, wondering if he'd caught Mark's

initial reaction. He met her gaze and quirked his eyebrow in question. Before she could answer, Mark spoke up.

"If that's what you want, Stace, I'm in." He glanced at Kristi and Jason. "But with one change, let's do it at my place."

Kristi studied her friend. "Are you sure, Mark? We wouldn't want to impose."

"Absolutely," he said definitely, reaching for Stacy's hand and looking deep into her eyes. "If Stacy wants friends and family for Christmas, then that's what she should have." Turning to the others, he added, "Plus, I just finished remodeling. This will give me a chance to show off the results."

CHAPTER 4

On Christmas Eve, Kristi and Jason arrived together, each carrying a plate of Christmas cookies. Kristi's came from an exchange Mattie Stebbings had arranged at the quilt shop, and Jason's were holiday treats provided by his staff at the sheriff's office.

After dressing up for their dinner at *Rizzoli's*, Kristi had opted for more casual attire for this at-home get-together, pairing a tunic length Christmas sweater with black leggings. Jason had also donned a Christmas sweater over a red turtleneck and blue jeans so new Kristi could still smell the dye.

Stacy met them at the door wearing a red velvet tunic, slim forest green trousers, and red ballet flats. Mark wore his usual jeans and plaid flannel shirt, but had added a red velvet Santa hat for the occasion.

"Come on in, you two," Mark said. "Let's get this party rolling!"

Stacy grinned. "He means, 'We're so glad you could come.'" She punched him playfully on the arm. "Mark will take your coats, and I'll take those plates of cookies."

"Sure," Mark muttered. "She gets the goodies while I get the down jackets."

Kristi laughed. "That's one way to make sure the cookies make it to the table."

"True enough," Mark said with a grin.

Jason rubbed his hands together. "So what are we eating?"

Kristi elbowed him. "Patience, Sheriff. We should at least sit down and visit for a few minutes."

Stacy joined them again in time to wave her hand and say, "Boys! Always hungry." She took Kristi's arm and led her through the living room and into the formal dining room. "We might as well eat first. We can talk after their rumbly tumblies have been filled."

Mark winked at Jason. "See why I love her? She understands me perfectly."

"I thought you were going to show off your house," Kristi called over her shoulder to Mark.

"Later," he said. "The house isn't going anywhere, but the food…" He picked up a plate and moved toward the buffet table, an avid gleam in his eye. "I've been drooling over this stuff all afternoon, but Stace wouldn't let me touch it until you two got here."

Jason nodded and grabbed a plate. "Torture," he said sagely. "My mom was a master at it."

Stacy giggled and took Kristi's arm. Together they walked back into the living room. "So this is the living area. Had you seen it before?" When Kristi shook her head, Stacy continued. "The fireplace and mantle have always been there, but a past owner had bricked it in and installed an electric fireplace. Mark yanked that out and restored the original rock work. They'd also painted the mantle; a real shame. We found beautifully grained oak beneath those layers of paint. He also ripped out carpeting and restored the original hardwood floors."

"So it's been more restoration than remodeling?" Kristi asked.

Stacy nodded. "Yes, in the main part of the house, but he also added a new master bedroom suite complete with private bath. He'll show you that later. For now, let's get some food before they eat it all."

"Works for me."

The buffet held simple but filling food. Sliced chicken and ham, potato salad, coleslaw, deviled eggs, a selection of sliced fruit, and the piece de resistance, cheese fondue surrounded by cubes of crusty bread.

After everyone had eaten their fill—and indulged in the plates of cookies, fudge, and chocolate cake—they carried their dishes to the kitchen where Kristi and Jason admired the new, stainless steel appliances, wrought iron baker's rack, and moveable work island.

"This is a great kitchen, Mark," Kristi praised. "It's perfect for baking and for entertaining."

"That's what I was going for," he agreed.

Jason frowned. "You're planning to entertain? I've gotta be honest, that never crosses my mind."

Mark put an arm around Stacy's waist. "Let's go back to the living room."

"But the food," Stacy began.

"We need to get it put away," Kristi finished.

"Later," Mark said firmly and propelled Stacy to the front of the house where he paused to light the fire he'd stacked earlier.

"Take a seat, everyone." He turned to Stacy. Taking her hands, he said, "I'd planned to do this privately, but you wanted Kristi and Jason here, so..."

Releasing her hands, Mark dropped to one knee, pulled a small velvet box from his pocket, and opened it to reveal a diamond solitaire. "Stacy Jean Akins, will you marry me?"

The only sound in the room was the crackling of the fire as the logs caught and burned brightly. Jason reached over and entwined his fingers with Kristi's while she held her breath, waiting for Stacy's response. She didn't have to wait long.

"Oh, Mark," Stacy whispered. She dropped to her knees beside him and when she raised her eyes to his, they brimmed with tears. "Of course I'll marry you."

Mark wrapped his arms around her and kissed her thoroughly.

When they broke apart, he took the ring from the box and placed it on the ring finger of her left hand. It fit perfectly.

Kristi and Jason sat perfectly still until the newly engaged couple stood and turned to them. Then Kristi ran to hug Stacy while Jason shook Mark's hand. All four of them beamed.

Kristi was busy admiring Stacy's stunning diamond solitaire set in yellow gold when Mark said, "You know, you were right, Stace. This *is* better with friends to share it with! Speaking of sharing…." He paused and grinned. "I've got another gift for Stacy, and I know Kristi's been dying to see this one!"

Jason and Stacy gave Kristi nearly identical quizzical glances, but she just shrugged. "This night is just full of surprises. What's next, Mark?"

"Come along and find out."

With that he led them down a hallway, past three lovely bedrooms and a fully remodeled bath to the new master bedroom suite. The room was dominated by a rustic king-size aspen log bed topped with a beautiful Christmas Star quilt. *Kristi's* Christmas Star quilt.

"Oh, Mark," Stacy breathed. "That bed is perfect. And that quilt… it's gorgeous!"

"Thank Kristi," Mark said, nodding to his friend. "She made it, just for you, though she didn't know it was for you when I commissioned it."

"Are you pleased with it, Mark?" Kristi asked quietly.

Mark smiled as he watched Stacy run her fingers lovingly over the beautifully stitched quilt. "What do you think?"

"I think," Jason said, pulling Kristi into his arms, "that you two are very lucky to have such a talented friend."

Mark nodded and turned to face Kristi. "It's perfect, Kristi." He took a deep breath before adding, "I wanted this quilt as a reminder for Stacy and me that our lives together started at Christmas. We may not get married until spring or summer, that'll be up to Stace, but everything starts right here, right now."

Stacy turned from her examination of the quilt, smiled brilliantly, and threw herself into Mark's arms. "This is the best Christmas EVER!"

Wish Fulfillment

A Short Sheriff Reynolds Mystery

DEBBIE MUMFORD

CHAPTER 1

The young man— hardly more than a boy really though he thought of himself as a man, had shouldered a man's responsibilities— guided the dark blue Subaru Outback along Interstate 90 toward Livingston, where he fully intended to head south on US 89 for Wyoming. Anything to get out and away from Montana.

Snow flurries blurred the landscape to an even gray and white, but that didn't worry him. Every Montanan knew how to drive in snow, and he was born and bred to the bone-deep chill of the state's winter weather.

He drove carefully, staying within the speed limit though he wanted to race the wind. Wouldn't do to be pulled over for speeding. Not while driving a stolen car. So he held his impulses in check and obeyed the law. For now.

Glancing to the right, he allowed his gaze to rest on his passenger. On the love of his short life. The moment he'd seen her in the shabby homeless shelter in Billings, he'd known she was the one. Since then he'd done everything he knew how to protect and provide for her. Including boosting this ride from the grocery store's frigid parking lot.

If they could just get out of Montana, everything would be

fine. They'd reinvent themselves, claim new identities. Get real jobs. Make a life together.

That was his Christmas wish— the only one he ever remembered making— to escape the hell of their past lives and start fresh somewhere else.

Anywhere else.

CHAPTER 2

Sheriff Jason Reynolds settled his official felt Stetson hat more firmly on his head as he stepped out of the single story white stucco building that housed the Garnet County Sheriff's Department. Studying the snow-covered length of Main Street, he allowed himself a moment of quiet pride. Garnet Gateway shone in the afternoon sun, pretty as a picturesque postcard. Diamond sparkles gleamed from the mounds of fresh snow, while evergreen wreaths with bright red bows decorated every street light, and colorful Christmas trees glowed in shop windows.

His town, the seat of his law enforcement jurisdiction, was a clean, quiet community, full of law-abiding citizens and all-around good people. He was a lucky man to have landed in this place. And luckier still to have earned the respect and trust needed to be elected Garnet County Sheriff.

Garnet Gateway was a far cry from the teeming streets of Denver, Colorado where he'd worked his way up from beat cop to homicide detective, and Jason was pleased and content with the difference. He'd learned a lot during his time in Denver, but he'd been relieved to return to his roots in rural Montana.

Pulling the collar of his sheepskin lined leather coat high

around his neck to combat the wind and swirling snow, he strode down the carefully shoveled sidewalk toward Garnet Gateway's one and only jewelry store. Christmas was right around the corner and he wanted something special for Kristi this year.

Kristi. Just thinking her name warmed his heart and put a smile on his lips. The woman might be his ex-wife currently, but she was the love of his life. And the last few months had given him cause to think she might agree to marry him again someday.

He'd been a fool. Had a fling at an out-of-state convention and had paid a heavy price. But he'd also learned the value of what he'd lost. If he ever convinced her to give him another chance, he wouldn't risk her love again.

He wanted to give her diamonds for Christmas, but knew they weren't there yet. Instead, he'd buy her something pretty, but not too precious. Something she could wear to work at her quilt shop… and think of him when she saw it or touched it. Maybe a necklace or a bracelet. Not a ring. The only rings he wanted to give her would signify engagement and marriage. But earrings? Yeah. Maybe a set of small, not too flashy diamond stud earrings.

Thinking of Kristi and an appropriate Christmas gift, he pulled the jewelry story door open and stepped inside, out of the blowing snow…

„„and into a robbery in progress.

CHAPTER 3

The scene before him froze, like some tableau in a waxworks museum. Edward Kauffman, the shop owner, stood behind the counter, his cheeks as red as any department store Santa, but it wasn't merriment that twinkled behind his thick, round, rimless glasses. It was pure, heart-pounding fear. A sheen of sweat glazed his forehead despite the room's winter chill.

Across the counter from Mr. Kauffman, a young couple huddled against the glass display case. The woman wore faded blue jeans, well-worn Sorel packs, and a puffy, dark blue down jacket that had seen too many winters. Stringy blonde hair escaped from a ragged black watch cap and her face was pinched with cold and probably hunger. The man wore similar clothes, though his head was covered with a tired-looking trapper hat with the ear flaps pulled down. He also looked like hearty meals were few and far between.

Jason might have been inclined to offer to buy the pair a meal, except for the fact that the man held a gun pointed straight at Mr. Kauffman's chest.

When the bell above the door tinkled and Jason stepped in, all three turned to stare at him. He took in the tableau, understood its meaning, and gauged his reaction before the door clicked shut behind him.

Smiling, he stepped forward, eyes on the shop owner. "Hey, Mr. Kauffman," he said, projecting as much calm as possible toward the frightened man. "I'm looking for a Christmas gift for Kristi. Figured you'd have just the thing."

Knowing his badge and gun were hidden beneath his sheep-skin coat, he stepped further into the room. Not as handy as he might wish if things went south, but not shouting 'law enforcement' either. Yanking his Stetson from his head, he dropped it on the closest display case with the emblem on its band angled away from the couple.

"You go right ahead, Mr. Kauffman. I can see you're busy with these nice folks." He nodded toward the young couple, his smile never wavering. "I'll just look around. Maybe something will strike my fancy."

The young man licked his lips, but straightened away from the display case, pulling the gun closer to his body and out of Jason's sight.

"That's right, Mr. Kauffman. Why don't we go on back and finish our business." He jerked his head toward a curtained alcove.

Jason knew the curtain led into the back of the store. He couldn't allow the gunman to remove the shop owner from the showroom. But how to stop him without resorting to a gun fight?

Still smiling, Jason strolled a few steps closer to the trio before stopping and glancing into a nearby display case. Good thing Mr. Kauffman's shop was a small one.

"Say there, miss," Jason said, aiming his smile at the young woman. "Since you're the only female here, would you mind giving me your opinion of this necklace? Too much? Or not enough? It's our first Christmas as a couple."

The woman jerked, surprised to be addressed, and turned a questioning gaze on her partner.

The man's eyes widened, then narrowed.

"Stay where you are, honey," he said, then turned his full attention to Jason, his gun hand in the pocket of his parka. "Why don't you mind your own, mister, or better yet, come back some other time."

Keeping his eyes on the jewelry beneath the glass, Jason sidestepped as close to the gunman as possible. Before the fellow could protest and order him back, Jason grabbed the man's gun arm, used his own hip as a fulcrum and tumbled the man to Mr. Kauffman's spotlessly clean black and white tile floor. The gun clattered from the man's pocket as he tried to catch his balance and get to his feet.

"Billy!" the woman screamed.

Jason kicked the gun out of the man's reach and pulled out his restraints. Kneeling, Jason cuffed the young man.

Billy struggled against Jason's hold, but managed to yell, "Run, Julie!"

Julie hesitated, then ran for the door.

Without even glancing up, Jason stuck out his leg and tripped her. She landed with a thump, sprawling out flat.

"Mr. Kauffman, please dial 9-1-1," Jason said calmly as he moved to restrain the woman. "Ask Deputy Millson to come give us a hand."

CHAPTER 4

Sheriff Jason Reynolds sipped black coffee from a chipped white mug as he studied the prisoners currently in his custody. He'd had Billy and Julie escorted from the detention center, a distance of two blocks, and settled in an interview room. He now stood in the narrow observation room, along with the county prosecutor Nancy Vanderhaven, a striking woman in her mid-sixties, with steel gray hair, pale blue eyes that missed little, and a wit as sharp as her intellect. They watched the couple through a two-way glass. Without their winter gear and wearing orange detention jumpsuits, Billy and Julie looked younger than he'd initially thought.

They'd declined to give him their full names at the time of arrest, but when he'd returned to his office he'd discovered an APB out of Billings listing them as William "Billy" Thompkins and Julie Monroe. The pair were 16-year-old runaways who had been living on the streets of Billings. They were now wanted for theft, grand theft auto, and unlawful possession of a firearm.

As far as Jason knew, their attempted theft at the jewelry story was the first time they'd used a weapon during a robbery. He'd contacted the Billings police and the two departments had agreed that since Garnet County had the pair in custody, Jason would retain jurisdiction. It would be up to Garnet County to determine justice.

After reading over their files, Jason had his own thoughts on what should be done with the pair, but he'd need the prosecutor to sign off on the deal. And everything would hinge on how the youngsters responded in interview.

Gulping the last of his coffee, he turned to the prosecutor. "Well, Ms. Vanderhaven, let's get this done. And hope these two have the sense to tell me the truth, and to recognize what's good for them if you agree with my idea."

"Agreed," she said, studying the young people on the other side of the glass. "I'll need them to show some remorse, give me some sense that they'll accept help, will make an effort to change their course."

He nodded. "We'll see what we see."

Setting his empty cup on a counter, Jason entered the interview room.

Glancing at the couple, he sat down across the scarred metal table from them and folded his hands.

"For the record this is Sheriff Jason Reynolds interviewing William "Billy" Thompkins and Julie Monroe." He paused, and looked each in the eye. "Have you both been read your rights and do you understand them?"

"Yes, sir," Billy said quietly. Julie simply nodded.

"Ms. Monroe, would you state that aloud, please?"

"Yes," she said, her voice quiet and defeated. "I understand."

Jason leaned back in his chair, extended his legs and crossed them at the ankles. "Good. Now that the formalities are out of the way, let's talk."

Billy met Jason's gaze, his expression confused. "Talk?"

Julie bit her lip and stared at the table. "What's there to talk about? You're sending us back, aren't you?" she asked quietly.

"Well, now, that's up to you two. I've read your files and from what I can see, you've had a rough time so far. We won't discuss why you ran away, you can talk that out with someone better qualified than me, but you need to know that Billings PD has agreed to let us deal with your brushes with the law up there. As long as proper restitution is made."

Both heads rose and two pair of wide eyes stared straight at him.

He nodded. "Good. I can see I have your attention now." He rose walked to a small wooden table in the corner where several bottles of water waited. Holding one up, he made a show of offering it to them, eyebrows raised. "You want one?"

"Yes, sir," they said in unison.

Gathering three bottles, he turned back to the metal table and handed two over. Uncapping his own, he took a long swallow.

"Now, what I need from you two is some answers. Why did you steal that car? Where were you headed? What did you plan to do when you got there? Answer straight and I may be able to help you instead of locking you up and sending you to trial."

Billy and Julie gazed into each other's eyes a moment, then Julie nodded. "You tell him," she said quietly.

Billy nodded, uncapped his water, took a swig, then settled the bottle on the table, both hands clutching it.

"Well, sir, it's like this. We ran away." He paused, licked his lips, and his eyes took on a glazed expression as though remembering something unpleasant. Then he shook himself and continued. "Different reasons, different places, different times. But we both ended up in Billings. Met at a homeless shelter, and recognized each other."

Jason frowned. "You knew each other before?"

Julie shook her head. "No. We just knew we belonged together." She shrugged. "Like from another life or something."

Billy nodded, his eyes bright. "I know it sounds crazy, but I just knew she was for me, and she felt the same... about me, I mean." He threw a shy smile in her direction, before clearing his throat. "Anyway, we teamed up. Tried to find work, but no one wanted to pay a couple of down-on-their-luck teens to do nuthin, and shelters fill up fast, especially in winter, and Julie was looking thin and poorly, so I decided we needed to get the hell out of Montana." His cheeks heated and he bobbed his head. "Sorry for cussin'."

"No problem," Jason said, keeping his face sober though he wanted to grin. "So you stole the car to get away from Billings?"

"Yes, sir."

"And the jewelry store? Why did you try to rob the jewelry store? Were you looking for something in particular?" Jason wondered if Billy had decided Julie needed a ring?

"Well, no, not really," Billy said, staring at the water bottle in his clasped hands. "We were almost out of gas, and I figured a jewelry store would have cash money. Then we could buy gas and keep right on driving to Wyoming."

Not what he'd expected, Jason thought. Not at all.

"So you were heading to Wyoming. Do you have family there? Someone to help you and take care of you?"

Julie shook her head, her stringy blonde hair falling like a shroud across her face.

"No, sir," Billy said. "But we thought, seein' as no one would know us there, we could make up new names, tell folks we were twenty or so, and get jobs. Make a home for ourselves."

"That's all we want," Julie whispered. "A home. It's almost Christmas and we wished for a home. Someplace. Anyplace. But we wanted to make a home. Be a family."

Billy put his arm around her, and pulling her close, touched his forehead to hers.

Jason leaned forward and crossed his arms on the table. "Is that the God's honest truth?" he asked.

They both nodded.

He slapped his hands on his knees and rose. "You two sit

tight," he said, and smiled at himself. As if they had any choice! "I need to have a conversation with someone, then we'll see what we can do with the pair of you."

He strode out of the room, closing the door firmly behind himself.

CHAPTER 5

"What do you think?" Jason asked Nancy Vanderhaven. "Are you willing to take a chance?"

Ms. Vanderhaven nodded. "Despite the gun, they hardly seem like hardened criminals, and I'd rather not toss them into institutions that could turn them into ones. I'm willing to sign off on your proposal, Sheriff, but I want you to monitor them closely. Don't let this get out of control."

Jason nodded. "Let me make a few calls, get everything lined up. I'll have the information for you later this afternoon."

They shook hands.

"Let's make this work, Sheriff."

CHAPTER 6

By the time Jason got back to them, Billy and Julie had been escorted back to the detention center, eaten lunch, had an hour or so in their bunks, and been escorted back to the interview room. When Jason stepped in, they both raised their faces to him, their eyes cautiously hopeful.

Jason resumed his seat across from them, crossed his arms on the table, and studied their faces. "Billy. Julie. I have an opportunity for you. It's up to you whether or not you accept, but I've got to be honest, if you don't the prosecutor will file charges against you for grand theft auto, attempted robbery, and unlawful possession of a firearm."

Julie lowered her head so her hair hid her face. Billy gulped audibly.

"I'm not trying to pressure you," Jason continued. "I just want to be sure you understand your choices." He waited a beat, then added, "And you don't have to make the same choice. Each of you can choose independently. Understand?"

They glanced at each other, and then nodded.

"First, if you accept this offer, Mr. Kauffmann has agreed to let the attempted robbery charge drop. No harm. No foul.

However, the Subaru will be returned to its owner in Billings and you two will be responsible for paying the county back for the delivery fee and repairs for any damage you caused."

Panic bloomed in Billy's eyes. "But, sir..."

Jason held up a hand. "Just wait until you've heard the whole thing, Billy."

The young man slumped in his chair, but nodded.

"Now, Billy. I've arranged for you to be fostered at the Broken M ranch. Carl Marsten will provide room and board and teach you about ranching. He'll also pay you a small salary for your work, part of which will be withheld until your debt to the county is cleared."

Billy opened his mouth, but Jason silenced him with a look.

"Julie, you'll be fostered here in town with the Kuhlmans. Silvi owns a bakery, and in addition to providing room and board, Silvi will teach you to bake— pies and cakes, that sort of thing— and will also give you a part-time job with a salary. Part of your wages will also go to your debt. You were part of this, so no reason Billy should pay it alone.

"You'll both attend school here in Garnet Gateway, and will be obliged to keep your grades reasonable and stay out of trouble. If you can manage all that, you'll be free to choose your own paths once you turn eighteen and graduate."

Billy's mouth worked, but no words came out. His face alternated between flushed and pale, and his eyes were wide as saucers. Julie looked completely gobsmacked.

Jason clapped his hands and stood. "I know it's a lot to think about, so I'll just leave..."

"No!" Billy practically shouted. "Don't go. Yes. I mean..." he scrubbed his face with both hands, glanced at Julie for confirmation, and continued, "I mean, for my part. I accept. I don't need to think about it. You might change your mind."

Jason's gaze softened. "No one will change their minds, Billy. Or for you, Julie. Garnet Gateway wants you to have a decent chance in life. I can't say this will be easy— ranching is hard work and bakers put in long hours— but it's a chance to learn a skill and live safe while you're learning." He smiled. "And nothing says the two of you can't go out on a date now and then."

Julie's eyes shone with tears. "I accept, Sheriff. Thank you."

"All right then. Let's get you two some decent clothes— you can't go to your new homes in detention jumpsuits— and I'll let your families know they can come and collect you."

Billy and Julie stood up and hugged each other. After a moment, Billy pulled back and grinned at Julie. "Did you hear that, honey? He said we had *homes*... and *families*!"

Julie nodded, and a tear rolled down her cheek. "It's our Christmas wish come true."

Jason grinned as he strode from the room to find Deputy Millson. He'd have her help the youngsters choose some clothes from the department's supply room. He had calls to make. Calls that would give two troubled teens a decent shot at life.

He still needed to find the perfect present for Kristi, but he wasn't worried. He'd helped make a Christmas wish come true. Finding a gift for the woman he loved would be a snap in comparison!

A MEMORABLE STROLL

CHAPTER 1

Chloe Walker experienced an interesting mix of exhaustion and exhilaration as she hurried along the snow packed street. The Christmas Stroll always had that effect on her. She worked herself until she could barely stand in the weeks leading up the annual holiday event—she was responsible for making sure everything ran smoothly, ensuring the community a memorable experience—but when the big day arrived, she received a jolt of energy from Main Street's festive atmosphere and the strollers' delighted chatter. That buzz always lasted until she fell into bed long after The Stroll's lights dimmed and all the revelers returned home.

This year, like every other year, Main Street was closed to traffic for the free community event. Folks would turn out in droves to stroll the six block stretch this evening, singing carols, munching cookies and candy canes, and buying last minute Christmas gifts. There would even be horse-drawn wagon rides available for those who tired of walking. Bright lights, festive decorations, and snow.

Lots of snow.

Chloe grinned. If there was one thing Bozeman, Montana could be counted on for, it was snow!

Pedestrian traffic was still light, but that would change soon. Chloe had only just finished supervising the gingerbread house decorating contest at the community center. Now a group of stalwart volunteers were moving the finished masterpieces to the Main Street bank lobby where strollers could marvel at the local children's ingenuity. Chloe was officially off duty for the rest of the evening. The Stroll would officially begin in a few minutes, and she intended to enjoy the event to the fullest.

Dressed in her warmest down jacket and ski pants, her fingers protected by warm woolen mittens knitted in a snowflake pattern, Chloe pulled her jacket's fur trimmed hood over her head, covering the matching knit cap. Her warm breath puffed out creating a tiny white cloud as it hit the cold late afternoon air. She patted her pocket, reassuring herself that her neck gaiter hadn't fallen out. She'd need it before the night was over; December in Montana was bitterly cold.

After her afternoon of kids and gingerbread, she craved a cup of steaming hot cider, and she knew just where to find it. She hurried past storefronts decorated in their holiday best—twinkling lights, plastic snowmen and reindeer, model trains circling ceramic villages, and of course Christmas trees, whether artificial or the real thing—aiming for her best friend's bookstore, *A Novel Experience*. Abbie always had hot spiced cider and fresh baked snickerdoodle cookies available during The Stroll.

Chloe had almost reached the warmth and light of *A Novel Experience* when someone bumped into her, almost knocking her to the ground. A pair of strong hands in leather work gloves steadied her and she glanced up into the concerned face of a man.

A man she knew.

A man she hadn't seen since high school and had frankly never expected to see again.

"I'm so sorry," he said, releasing her as soon as she was stable on her feet. "I wasn't watching…" He stopped and peered into her face. "Chloe? Is that you? I don't believe it."

"Hi, Alex," she said. "What brings you back to Bozeman?"

"The holidays," he said with a smile. A very disarming smile. Chloe's blood raced, the roar in her ears almost making her miss the rest of his comment. "…and family, of course."

Pulling herself together and hoping the brisk, cold breeze would explain away the red she could feel heating her cheeks, Chloe responded with, "Of course." Glancing at the brightly decorated bookstore window, she asked, "Does Abbie know you're back?"

Alex shook his head, the mischievous grin that Chloe remembered all too well lighting his eyes. "I stopped by the ranch to see Mom and Dad and drop off my duffle bag. Mom wanted to call Abbie immediately, but when she said Abbie was working the Christmas Stroll tonight, I swore them to secrecy." He paused and, if possible, his grin got even wider. "I mean, seriously? How often do I have the chance to sneak up on my womb-mate?"

Chloe giggled. An actual, school-girl giggle! Alex's use of that bizarre term for his twin sister—and her best friend—had always had that effect on her.

"Well come on then," she said, pulling him toward the door. "I can't wait to see her reaction."

But he planted his feet, becoming an immovable object, and shook his head. "You go first. I don't want to *totally* overwhelm her." He shook a finger at her, but ruined the effect by grinning again. "Just don't give away my surprise."

Chloe crossed her heart with mittened fingers. "Your secret is safe with me."

Crossing the snowy sidewalk in a few strides, Chloe paused at the door, glanced back at Alex with a grin, then took a deep breath to compose herself and stepped into *A Novel Experience*.

~

CHAPTER 2

As Alex watched Chloe disappear into his twin sister's bookstore a mixture of relief and excitement flooded his heart and mind. He couldn't believe his luck! He'd bumped into Chloe (literally!) on his own. He hadn't needed to beg his sister's or his mother's intervention. Either of them would've happily invited Chloe to some holiday event—they loved the woman like she was part of the family—but then he would've had to explain that a desire to see Chloe was a big part of the reason he'd finally made it home for Christmas this year, and as a man accustomed to keeping his own council, he'd rather not divulge that information.

Now that the ice had been broken, he could contact Chloe on his own, without the help of his nosey, if loving, sister, or his equally nosey, though infinitely loving, mother. His mission to determine if Chloe was still happily married or if the tantalizing hints his sister had dropped—but failed to verify—were true and the woman of his dreams was once again on her own would succeed or fail on its own merits…without undue familial interference.

Nodding to himself, he set his goals for Chloe aside and

prepared to face the whirlwind that was his vivacious and talented twin sister, Abbie.

CHAPTER 3

The moment Chloe stepped inside, the warmth of *A Novel Experience* engulfed her like a long overdue hug. Early though it was, quite a few people milled around the shelves of Abbie's bookstore surrounded by sparkling lights, scents of apples, cinnamon and fresh-cut pine, and soft Christmas music. The owner herself stood behind the refreshment table filling insulated cups with mulled cider and encouraging her customers to enjoy a snickerdoodle.

Chloe caught her friend's glance and waved, hoping to lure her away from the hot cider. It would be just like Alex to sneak up behind Abbie and surprise her into tossing a cup of the hot liquid into the air. *That* kind of surprise wasn't one Chloe wanted to see.

As hoped, Abbie handed off the cider duty to one of her employees and hurried across the shop to give Chloe a hug.

"What are you up to, Chloe?" she asked as they broke apart and she held her friend at arms' length. "You look absolutely breathless."

Chloe could only hope her cheeks didn't add any more color at her friend's insightful comment. Taking Abbie's arm, Chloe led her into a quiet corner, away from the crowd at the refreshment table. "Oh, you know," she said, lowering her hood and unzipping her down jacket, "it's cold out there. Plus, I just finished helping the kids build their gingerbread houses." She laughed. "Talk about hectic!"

Abbie rolled her eyes. "I can only imagine...thank heavens! Just think, next year you'll have to deal with Jilly and Jerry!"

Twins, especially the boy-girl variety, seemed to run in Abbie's family. Her own kids were too young for the gingerbread house competition this year, but next year...watch out! Jilly and Jerry would be covered in frosting just like the rest of the kids.

Before Chloe could respond, the bell over the door jingled and Abbie turned to see who had come in...and saw Alex.

For an instant, Chloe thought her friend might faint—the color drained from Abbie's face and the hand she raised to her lips trembled, but then she squealed and launched herself across the room and into Alex's arms. While her best friend cried and bounced and swatted Alex for not telling her he was coming home, Chloe sauntered over to the refreshments and claimed the cup of mulled cider she'd been craving. Taking a sip, she closed her eyes and savored the warmth and comfort of the perfectly spiced drink. Apples, of course, with just the right amount of cinnamon, cloves, and orange peel. Truly, a seasonal favorite. Especially since Abbie always brewed hers with locally pressed cider.

Before Chloe could finish that first cup of cider, Abbie stopped bouncing and composed herself. Grabbing Alex's arm, she dragged him over to join Chloe before swatting him on the shoulder.

"You know I can't leave the shop during The Stroll," she said with an accusatory glare. "You planned it this way."

Alex laughed, a warm, deep rumble. "Maybe. But you couldn't expect me to miss The Stroll just because you have to work, could you?"

Abbie rolled her eyes, but her expression showed nothing but delight. "I suppose not." Turning to Chloe, she said, "Keep an eye on him, will you, Chloe? I don't want him disappearing before I get a chance to visit with him properly."

"Hey, now," Alex protested. "I'm home for the holidays. Chloe doesn't need to babysit me." Then he cocked his head and winked at Chloe. "Unless you *want* to babysit me, that is."

Chloe blushed, her fair skin turning even pinker than the frigid temperature outdoors had caused. She opened her mouth to respond, but nothing came out. Alex's sudden appearance after so many years of absence had robbed her of witty banter. Quickly, she took another sip of hot cider allowing the warmth to soothe her while the tart flavor cleared her mind.

Ignoring Alex's teasing comment, she turned to Abbie. "He's not going anywhere, Abbs. Not without seeing your folks and Ed and the kids, but," she slid her gaze sideways to the man in question, "I'll be happy to stroll with him, if he'd like."

There. She'd lobbed the metaphorical ball straight back to him. Where it belonged.

Alex laughed again, and Chloe thought she could get used to that distinctly masculine rumble. "Caught in my own net." He waved to his sister and held out a hand to Chloe. "Come on then. Let's see what Bozeman has to offer these days."

～

CHAPTER 4

Main Street had never looked so good to Alex.

The Christmas Stroll was in full swing, the street filling with happy crowds. Excited children dashed from display to display, while their parents alternately called out cautions and chatted with friends. Shops were packed so tightly customers could hardly move, but no one minded. Christmas spirit ruled, plus there were free brownies and cookies and cider for all.

Just from a moment's observation Alex could tell the event was a huge success, but after that first glance, he hardly noticed the lights and gaiety. He was in a daze. A Chloe Walker induced daze. He couldn't believe his luck. Not only had he literally bumped into Chloe, but Abbie had provided the perfect impetus he'd needed to talk Chloe into spending some time with him.

And now, here he was, strolling through Bozeman's frigid winter weather enjoying the holiday sights and sounds with the woman he'd dreamed about since high school. If only the hints Abbie had dropped were true and Chloe was single again. He shook himself. Married or not, he would enjoy this precious time with her.

They were standing in front of the hardware store admiring

the model train circling a village of ceramic buildings when Chloe turned to him. "So," she said, "where have you been all these years? What's up with you?"

"You know I joined the Marines right out of high school, right? That's kept me busy. Still does, as a matter of fact."

"You're still on active duty?"

"Yep. Home on leave for the holidays."

She nodded, but changed the subject. "I can't believe I haven't seen you since high school. How have I managed to miss your other visits?"

"Well, let's see now." He tapped his chin with a leather gloved finger. "The first time I came home, you were in Seattle. I think Abbie said you'd followed a guy you met at university."

She narrowed her eyes and hissed. "I did *not* follow him! I was just there for a visit."

"Ri-ight," he drawled the word out, giving her a knowing smirk. "The next time you were hiking in Yellowstone. With another guy." He grinned, but then his expression grew serious. "The next thing I heard, you were married. To the Yellowstone guy?"

Chloe sighed. "Yes. Jeremy and I married just a few months after Abbie married Ed." She paused, tilted her head, and met his gaze. "I was surprised you didn't come home for her wedding."

He shrugged. "Couldn't. My team was deployed."

A little frown creased her brow. "Really? Where?"

Wiggling his eyebrows and twirling a nonexistent mustache, he said, "I could tell you, but then I'd have to…"

She laughed and raised a hand. "Stop. I get the picture." Shaking her head, she led him into the hardware store to warm up with a cup of hot chocolate and a brownie.

"So what about you?" she asked. "Married with kids like your sister?"

He paused with the remains of his second brownie halfway to his mouth. "Seriously? You think I'd've shown up at the

Christmas Stroll alone if I had a wife and kids?" He shook his head. "Just because you're an independent woman whose husband doesn't mind you wandering around without him doesn't mean I'd leave my wife alone while I came home to Bozeman."

She glanced aside and said quietly, "Jeremy and I divorced two years ago"

Alex's heart swelled with satisfaction, but her demeanor tempered his delight. Wiping his fingers on a napkin, he reached for her hand. "Chloe, I'm sorry. Abbie didn't tell me."

"No reason she should have," Chloe said. Disentangling their fingers, she tossed her empty cup in the trash and pulled her mittens back on. "Come on. Let's go see the gingerbread houses."

~

CHAPTER 5

A few minutes later, Alex and Chloe stood in the lobby of the bank examining the gingerbread house exhibit. Studying the local children's creations gave Chloe the space she needed to wrestle her growing attraction to her best friend's twin brother into perspective. When he'd taken her hand in the hardware store, the sizzle of chemistry between them had nearly made her spill the remains of her hot chocolate. She was reacting to Alex like she hadn't to any man since she'd divorced Jeremy. Truth be told, her visceral reaction to Alex was a magnitude greater than anything she'd ever felt for her ex-husband.

But regardless of the butterflies currently swarming in her stomach, she needed to be calm and cool-headed. Alex was just home for a visit. He'd be leaving soon and her life would go on as it had for the last two years. She'd made a good life for herself. This attraction to Alex was simply an aberration.

She managed to tune back in to the current conversation in time to hear him say, "I don't know. I know you like that Victorian with the frosted trees and the skating pond made out of blue sprinkles, but I'm partial to that little log cabin over there." He pointed to a very simple confection, constructed to look like stacked logs with icicles of white frosting dripping from a roof shingled with light gray wafer candies.

"Well, I may be biased since I supervised the contest and watched all of these houses being built." She smiled up at him, still surprised by how tall he'd gotten. The last time she'd seen him, he'd still been a gawky teen, not yet grown into his full height. He'd still had that puppy-ish look of hands and feet too large for his body.

But this Alex...well, there was nothing immature about the man beside her. This was a well-built, adult male in his prime who filled out his down jacket and denim jeans very nicely.

"You wouldn't believe how hard the kids worked on these. Their concentration and attention to detail was impressive."

Chuck nodded. "I can see that. These are a lot better than the ones I remember making."

She laughed. "Yes, but you were always more interested in eating frosting than in building a house."

"Guilty as charged," he agreed, his eyes sparkling.

Just then the horse-drawn wagon rattled past the bank, filling the air outside with the sounds of sleigh bells and laughter.

"That looks like fun," Alex said. "Want to go for a ride?"

Chloe froze, her mouth dry and her heart pounding. He was talking about a wagon ride, she knew he was talking about a wagon ride, but her traitorous hormones hijacked her brain and dragged it in an entirely different direction. Forget horses with bells on their harness, Chloe wanted nothing more than to have a ride...an amorous ride!...with this handsome, virile man.

She shivered and dragged her mind back to The Stroll. A family friendly, decidedly non-sexy, holiday event.

Pasting on a *we're just friends* smile, she nodded. "That would be great!"

They hurried to the wagon stop two storefronts down from the bank where the gingerbread houses were displayed and got in line.

"We timed that right," Alex said, nodding to the approaching wagon.

After a quick head count of the line ahead of them, Chloe grinned. Being one of the event's organizers had its perks. She knew the wagon's capacity. No waiting for them! They'd be able to find seats on this one.

When their turn came, Alex handed Chloe up into the wagon and then sat down beside her. Very close beside her. He put his arm around her and drew her closer still. She stiffened, then relaxed. Even if he would only be in Bozeman for a few days, she could allow herself to enjoy cuddling in a horse-drawn wagon during The Christmas Stroll. She'd worked hard on this event; she'd guard her heart later. Right now, she just wanted to enjoy the moment.

Resting her head on Alex's shoulder, she savored the holiday spectacle. Swirling snowflakes blurred the colorful lights and festive decorations, giving Main Street a magical glow. People bundled in their winter coats and hats exhaled little white clouds as they chatted and sang. Children raced from back and forth across the snow-packed street, enjoying its car-less condition. The Stroll was a success and she was snuggled safe and warm in Alex Campbell's arms.

All was right in her world.

∼

CHAPTER 6

Alex had been savoring the moment. Chloe snuggled against his side, her head resting on his shoulder. The perfect end to a perfect Stroll.

But then the wagon stopped and they had to get down so the next folks could have their turn. Bummer. He could've stayed in that wagon forever, frozen in time.

His timing had always been off where Chloe was concerned. She was either in a relationship or he was deployed to the far side of the world. But this time, this time fate had given him a break. Chloe was single again—he'd have words with Abbie for not confirming that information for him—and he was home for the holidays. And the spark he'd felt since high school? That spark was rapidly growing into a flame. At least, it was for him.

But what about Chloe? Did she feel it too?

He raised his arms to help Chloe out of the wagon. As he lifted her down, their eyes met, and electricity practically sparkled in the cold wintry air. Her eyes widened, and he knew.

She felt it too.

Pulling her away from the line of folks waiting to board the wagon, Alex stopped in an unlit doorway.

"Alex," she whispered, her voice little more than a breath.

"Chloe, listen..." he stammered, his heart beating too fast to allow the words to flow.

"Shhh." She rose up on tiptoe and kissed him. Not a passionate kiss, but one that held a world of promise. "The wagon ride was the perfect end to our evening." Taking his hand, she asked, "Walk me to my car?"

"It would be my pleasure."

She led him to the parking lot and her bright red Subaru Outback. "I need to get home," she said quietly. "I have a lot to think about."

He nodded and opened the driver's door for her. "May I call you tomorrow?"

She smiled. "I'll be disappointed if you don't." She paused, then lifted a mittened hand to his cheek. "You're what I'll be thinking about."

Alex watched as Chloe maneuvered her car carefully out of the snow covered parking lot. As soon as she was out of sight, he punched his fist in the air and gave a shout of victory. He'd call her tomorrow, and, if he had anything to say about it (and he intended to say a lot!) he'd spend the rest of his life with her.

This had been the most important night of his life. He and Chloe might just have to make The Stroll a Christmas tradition!

UNCOLLECTED ANTHOLOGY

MYSTICAL MAPS

ISSUE 32 UA DECEMBER 2023

FLIGHT PLAN

DEBBIE MUMFORD

CHAPTER 1

My cell phone buzzed. I glanced at the readout and sighed. Ethel Douglass. I was taking a well-deserved day off and the last thing I wanted was for Mrs. D, a seemingly sweet little old lady from Seattle, to tell me we were in for another supernatural invasion. I'd had enough ghouls and demons to last a lifetime.

My name is Gus Collier, and in addition to being a homicide detective for the city of Portland, Oregon, I'm also a seventh-seventh. The proverbial seventh son of a seventh son.

Not that gender has anything to do with it.

Seventh-seventh is a birth order anomaly. The seventh child of a seventh child is hard-wired to come into some form of psychic power. Usually on their twenty-eighth birthday. See, it's all about the sevens, and since twenty-eight is seven quadrupled, that's when it happens. Personally, I think putting it off until the seventh-seventh turns forty-nine (seven squared) would make even more sense, but no one asked my opinion.

I'm just living this weirdness.

Anyway, Mrs. Douglass is another seventh-seventh, but her abilities are different than mine. She uses higher mathematics to delve into the mysteries of alternate realities. As far as I've figured out, seventh-sevenths come in one of three types: guardians like me and my friend Luke; healers like my ghostly partner Sarah and our friend Alex; and those who are attuned to alternate realities, especially the Otherworld, like Ethel Douglass. All of us are psychic, so we can all see and hear Sarah, which makes life a whole lot easier when we're on a mission.

A mission. Just what I didn't need.

But I couldn't very well blow Mrs. D off, so I took a deep breath and answered her call.

"Hey, Mrs. D," I said, making a valiant attempt to sound bright and cheerful. After all, it was the week before Christmas, so *merry and bright* was all the rage. "What's up?"

"Good evening, Gus," she answered, her voice very crisp and proper. "I'm in Portland with a… *friend*… and I'd like to drop by. Is now convenient?"

It wasn't, but I didn't like the emphasis she'd placed on the word *friend*. Was Mrs. D in trouble? Did she need rescuing? My guardian hackles rose. No one would dare threaten Mrs. D! Not on my turf.

"Sure, Mrs. D. Come on by, but I warn you, it's been a long week and the place is a mess."

"Not to worry, Gus. We're not coming to inspect your house-keeping." Relief colored her words. "And, thank you." With that unexpected comment, she ended the call.

Sarah, my ghostly partner, floated over to join me on the couch.

What did Mrs. Douglass want? Sarah asked, her words flowing through my mind like cool water.

"She's coming over," I said, still staring at the cell phone in my hand, "and she's bringing a friend."

I glanced up at Sarah. She'd been a beauty in life— perfect peaches and cream complexion, large blue eyes, silky blonde hair — and despite being doomed to wear blue hospital scrubs with her hair pulled back in a pony tail for eternity, the woman was still perfect in my estimation.

I know. Sad and a little creepy to realize I was in love with a ghost, but the heart wants what the heart wants. Even if that desire is a physical impossibility.

"Something's weird. She didn't give me any details, but it's not like her to just drop by. Especially not with a friend. And since when does she drive down from Seattle without Alex? He usually acts as her chauffeur and she didn't even mention him."

Before Sarah could respond a buzzer sounded, letting me know that someone in the apartment building's lobby wanted access to the elevator. I jumped off the couch and strode to my door to answer the summons.

"Collier here."

"It's me, Gus," Mrs. D's voice responded.

I released the elevator. "Come on up. Sarah and I are ready and waiting."

A few moments later, she knocked on the door. I knew it was her without bothering to check the peephole— psychic, remember?— but whoever was with her remained a mystery. I could sense a presence, but couldn't bring a vision to mind. Frowning, I opened the door.

"Thank you for seeing us on such short notice, Gus." Mrs. D sailed past me into the living room, a small— make that *very* small— man dressed in a dark blue business suit in her wake. I closed the door and followed them.

"Gus. Sarah," Mrs. D said, nodding to each of us. "This is Smee. He has a problem that I believe the three of us can assist him with."

The little man scanned me from head to toe, then turned his gaze on Sarah.

Okay. That was unusual. Most normal folk aren't aware of Sarah. Can't see her, don't know she exists. At the very least, this little guy was psychic. Since he'd arrived with Mrs. D, he might not even be from this plane of existence.

Might as well start finding out what was what.

"Smee," I said. "Wasn't that the name of Captain Hook's first mate?"

He frowned at me, clearly not following my reference.

"You know," I clarified, "from Peter Pan."

"Sorry," he said after a long pause. His voice was unusually deep for such a small fellow. I'd expected something high and thin. "I'm not following you."

I sighed. "Never mind. Smee is just an unusual name in my experience."

He nodded. "That would be because it isn't a name. It's my designation. An acronym, if you will. S-M-E-E. Subject Matter Expert Elf. I'm Santa's logistical expert."

My knees turned to jelly and I plopped onto the couch. "You're what?"

Mrs. D settled herself in my recliner and Smee climbed onto the overstuffed chair across from her. "Really, Gus," Mrs. D said. "You'd think you'd never encountered unusual, uhm, people, before. Smee contacted me through my studies, my alternate realities computations, and asked for assistance. I brought him to you." She paused and gave me a stare that said *get control of yourself, young man* before continuing. "He's lost something valuable and you're a detective. So... detect!"

I closed my eyes, swallowed, and pulled myself together. At least Mrs. D wasn't in danger, and an elf who worked for Santa was a lot easier to deal with than a ghoul or a demon. Whatever this was, I could deal with it.

At least, I hoped I could.

CHAPTER 2

When I finally opened my eyes, nothing had changed. Mrs. D still sat in my recliner without having bothered to extend the footrest. Smee, Santa's putative elf, rested in the overstuffed chair, his booted feet not even reaching the edge of the cushioned seat. And Sarah hovered beside me on the couch.

All right then. Not a figment of my imagination.

"My apologies, Mr. Smee," I said leaning forward and planting my elbows on my knees, hands clasped in front of me. "How can I help?"

"Drop the mister," he replied. "It's just Smee."

I nodded. "Fine. How can I help, Smee?"

"Someone stole Santa's flight plan and I need it back. ASAP."

"There's some urgency about this, Gus," Mrs. D added. "Christmas is only a few days away and Yule begins at sunset tonight."

I glanced from one of them to the other. Christmas I understood, but what this had to do with Yule, I wasn't sure. And what the heck was Santa's flight plan?

"Okay," I said, deciding to ask my questions in what I hoped was a logical order. "I understand that whatever this *flight plan* is,

Santa needs it by Christmas Eve, but what's that got to do with Yule?"

Smee turned to glare at Mrs. D. "I thought you said he was a seventh-seventh, not just some uneducated human."

I bristled at the insult, but before I so much as opened my mouth, Mrs. D responded.

"He's young, Smee. This is his first Yule with power."

Smee sighed and turned back to me. "Yule is one of the old holy days. Santa derives his power from Yule, the winter solstice, from the returning light. He doesn't make his flight *during* the solstice because people's belief in him is tied to the newer Christmas holiday, but without the power of Yule, his reindeer wouldn't be able to fly and he wouldn't be able to stretch time to accommodate his extensive schedule."

I nodded. "Got it. Now, what's this missing flight plan?"

"It's Santa's map," Smee said, his deep voice reminding me of a croaking bullfrog. "The flight plan not only tells him where to go, but also the most efficient route. After all, he has a lot of stops to make in as short a time as possible."

"A map," I said with a frown. "You're his logistical expert, can't you just make him a new one?"

Smee's eyebrows rose so high I feared they'd get lost in his hairline.

"Just…just…make him a new one?" he spluttered. An angry red flush stained his cheeks and he rolled out of the chair and advanced on me. "No, I can't make him a new one! His flight plan isn't just a map! It's a magical artifact! It keeps track of every child in the world, adapting as they move from place to place, removing them as they age off, adapting to whether or not they've lost their belief. The flight plan is priceless! And without it Santa will be unable to fulfill the dreams of the world's children!"

He didn't say *you idiot*, but I heard the words nonetheless.

CHAPTER 3

While Smee calmed himself, Mrs. D drew me aside. Sarah floated over to join us.

"I think it best if I take Smee with me," Mrs. D said quietly. "We'll be at my usual suite at The Benson if you need us." She paused and glanced at the elf. "I'm not sure how we're supposed to find this flight plan, but Smee is attuned to it. I'll run some calculations and see if I can use his connection to the map to locate it." She smiled wryly. "I'll let you know what I find."

I nodded. "Sorry I got him all worked up." Shrugging I continued. "I haven't got a clue how to find this thing, but Sarah and I will put our heads together. Who knows? Maybe we'll get lucky."

I gave Mrs. D a spare key to the apartment and the code to the elevator so she wouldn't have to ring me for permission to come up and they left. Smee had calmed down enough to shake my hand, though he didn't look particularly happy about it.

When the door closed behind them, I collapsed on the couch.

"Well, that was fun," I said to Sarah. "Any ideas on how to find this magical map?"

Sarah settled on the end of the couch. She didn't really sit since she couldn't touch physical objects, but she managed to appear to snuggle into the cushions.

Not really. I mean, how do they expect us to find something we've never even seen? At least Mrs. Douglass has Smee to work with... and he at least knows what the map looks like as well as what it does.

"Agreed," I said. After a moment's pause, I had a thought. "I wonder why Smee contacted Mrs. D? And why come to Portland? I mean, he had the whole world to choose from and our little team can't be the only seventh-sevenths in the world."

Sarah shrugged her cute little insubstantial shoulders. *Maybe his connection to the map led him to the Pacific Northwest. Maybe she knows the map is in Portland.*

"Maybe. Do you think he knows who stole it?"

Possibly, but if so, wouldn't he have told us? Suddenly her eyes widened and her mouthed formed a sweet little "O." She rose into the air and floated toward the door. *Come on, Gus,* she cried. *I think I know where to look!*

I grabbed my keys from the hook by the door and followed her into the hall, pausing only to lock the apartment door.

"Where are we going?"

To my old stomping grounds, Sisters of Mercy Hospital.

I raced my department issued dark blue sedan through the streets of Portland and into the hospital's parking garage. From there I followed Sarah through a maze of corridors and elevators to the children's ward.

"What are we doing here, Sarah?" I whispered, trying not to move my lips so the people we passed wouldn't think I was talking to myself.

I was right, she said with a satisfied smile. *Look.*

Frowning at her, I shifted my gaze down the hall and saw a small female surrounded by a sparkle of magic. The way the doctors and nurses walked around her without seeming to see her told me she wasn't a normal person. As we got closer, I realized she was another elf. A female counterpart to Smee.

Even tinier than Smee, she was dressed in a red tunic and green tights. Her white-blonde hair was pulled into two pigtails and tied with red and green ribbons. She stood just outside a room with a single bed, staring through the glass door at a little girl in frilly pink pajamas. The child was bald, listless, and wan, her complexion nearly as pale as the pillows she rested against.

Is she the reason you stole the flight plan? Sarah asked.

The little female jumped, her startled gaze moving between Sarah and me for a moment before returning to the child. She nodded.

"I didn't steal it, not really," she said quietly. "I just borrowed it."

Have you done what you needed to do? The elf nodded again. *Then let's go back to Gus's apartment. You can tell us your story there.*

Talk about a weird experience. If you haven't driven across a busy city in the middle of the holiday season with a ghost and a silent elf, you have no idea what you're missing.

It was nearly sunset by the time we settled into my living room. Sarah and I took the couch and the little elf climbed into the overstuffed chair that Smee had occupied earlier. Evidently its cushy seat appealed to elves.

"Now," I said, "who are you and why did you steal the flight plan?"

"I didn't *steal* it," she said vehemently. "I only borrowed it. I intended to have it back before anyone even knew it was missing."

"Well, you failed on that point," I said. "Smee is here and he's fuming mad."

You didn't tell us your name, Sarah pointed out. *And I'd like to know what you were doing outside that little girl's room.*

"Good points," I said with a nod. "Who are you and what's your story?"

The elf closed her eyes and emitted a long sigh. "I'm called

Dolly because making dolls for children is my reason for existence. I borrowed the flight plan because I needed to see Bitsy."

She opened her eyes and met first my gaze, then Sarah's.

"You see, Bitsy asked for a doll, a very special doll, and since her name wavered in and out of existence on my list, I knew that this would be her last gift from Santa. Bitsy will have moved on to heaven before Christmas comes next year, so I wanted to be sure that the doll I made for her would fulfill her every dream."

Dolly paused, licked her lips, and sighed again.

"In order to be sure I made the perfect doll for her, I needed to see Bitsy. So I borrowed the flight plan and asked it to bring me here."

I stared at the little elf in amazement. I had absolutely nothing to say. This wasn't a crime and Dolly wasn't a criminal. No matter how mad Smee might be, Dolly had acted out of compassion and a desire to fulfill a dying child's dream. No way was I going to rebuke her.

You need to give the map back to Smee, Sarah said softly.

"No," Dolly said with a shake of her head, making her little white-blonde pigtails dance. "That's your job. I have to get back to Santa's workshop and make Bitsy's doll."

Having said that, she rolled out of the overstuffed chair and strode to Sarah. Without another word, she pulled a piece of yellowed parchment from her pocket and placed it in Sarah's hands.

But I can't... Sarah began, but the map didn't fall through her insubstantial fingers. No, her fingers began to glow and that glow crept up her hand to her wrist before continuing up her arm. As the glow progressed, Sarah changed from a ghostly shadow to a living, breathing woman.

Dolly smiled. "Even a ghost— and the man who loves her— deserves a gift of Yule magic."

Her words still hung in the air as Dolly disappeared in a shower of magical sparkles.

I stared open-mouthed at the place where she'd stood, then leapt to Sarah's side. Grabbing her hands, I pulled her into my arms, savoring the feel of her body pressed against mine, delighting in the beat of her heart, the flush of pink in her cheeks.

"Sarah," I whispered. "Happy Yule." For it was indeed Yule. The sun had set just as Dolly handed the map to Sarah. The elf's gift to Sarah, to both of us really, was this fleeting moment of substantiation.

"Happy Yule, indeed," Sarah said with a sigh just before our lips met.

If I could, I would've frozen time in that moment. Sarah, alive and breathing, in my arms. The two of us locked in a kiss that expressed all the pent-up passion our normal state couldn't relieve.

Unfortunately, I wasn't Santa. I didn't have the magic necessary to extend time.

We were still enjoying that amazing, unexpected kiss when Mrs. D and Smee unlocked the door and let themselves in.

EPILOGUE

When we finally emerged from the bliss of our Yule kiss, Sarah and I acknowledged Mrs. D and Smee. We resumed our earlier places, Mrs. D in the recliner, Smee in Dolly's recently vacated overstuffed chair, and Sarah and I on the couch, almost fused together from shoulder to hip, arms wound around each other's waists.

"We have the flight plan," Sarah told the other two. "An elf named Dolly borrowed it."

"Borrowed?" Smee asked, his voice so loud it could almost be classified as a shout.

"Yes," I said. "Borrowed. She expected to return it before anyone noticed it was missing."

Smee frowned, his whole face looking like it might break into a storm complete with thunder and lightning. Looking at him, I understood why Dolly had declined to return the map to him herself.

"I don't suppose she told you why she would do such a terrible thing," he growled.

"She needed it to visit a dying child," Sarah said calmly. "A little girl who asked for a special doll. A little girl who will never see another Christmas. Dolly wanted to make sure she fulfilled the child's dreams, that the doll she made for Bitsy would be exactly right."

The anger and righteous indignation drained from Smee's face. "Oh," he said quietly.

Silence descended, only to be broken a few moments later by Mrs. D.

"And how is it that Sarah is… corporeal?"

Sarah laughed. "Dolly's Yule gift to us," she said, glancing at me.

I kissed her cheek and then turned to Mrs. D with a nod. "She used her Yule magic to give us these few moments just before she disappeared. Said she was going back to Santa's workshop to make Bitsy's doll."

"Well," Smee said, "if you'll just hand over the map, we'll be on our way. I'm sure you two would like some privacy."

Sarah's pretty pink cheeks paled. "You don't think…"

The blood drained from my face as well. "I don't know."

"What?" asked Mrs. D and Smee together.

I gazed at the map still clutched in Sarah's hand. "It's just that Sarah's transformation started the moment the map touched her fingers."

"Oh," said Smee.

"Will I go back to being a ghost if I let go of the map?"

"I don't know," Smee admitted. "But I can't leave without the flight plan." He rolled out of the chair and moved to stand beside Sarah, hand outstretched.

"Of course," she said.

"Wait," I cried, jumping to my feet and pulling Sarah with me. I enveloped her in a desperate hug as I whispered, "At least let us have one more kiss."

Our lips met, melding our hearts and souls in a passion that could never be fulfilled. Before the kiss ended, Sarah dropped her hand to her side and released the flight plan into Smee's care. I felt the change begin. A tingling sensation that spread from her fingers to her wrist to her shoulder, and eventually stole her from my arms.

Tears stung my eyes, but I was aware of the front door clicking closed as Mrs. D and Smee left us to our grief... and the shining memory of Dolly's all-to-brief Yule gift.

Happy Yule indeed.

ALSO BY DEBBIE MUMFORD

Kristi Lundrigan Mysteries:

- DELECTABLE MOUNTAIN QUILTING (NOVEL)
- IN A PICKLE (NOVEL)
- DOUBLE WEDDING RING (NOVEL)
- FOOL'S PUZZLE (SHORT STORY)
- WILDFIRE! (SHORT STORY)
- CHRISTMAS STAR (SHORT STORY)

Sheriff Reynolds Mysteries:

- ABDUCTED! (NOVEL)
- WISH FULFILLMENT (SHORT STORY)

Gus and Ghost Short Story Series:

- SEVENTH
- SEVENTH: FIRST FRUITS
- DEATH OF AN ALCHEMIST (UNCOLLECTED ANTHOLOGY)
- SEVENTH: THE SAMHAIN DILEMMA
- DARK OF THE MOON (UNCOLLECTED ANTHOLOGY)
- FLIGHT PLAN (UNCOLLECTED ANTHOLOGY)
- MIDSUMMER NIGHT (UNCOLLECTED ANTHOLOGY)

Logans of Lastalrig Series:

- HER HIGHLAND LAIRD (NOVELLA)
- HER HIGHLAND YULE (SHORT STORY)
- WISE WOMAN (SHORT STORY)

Red's Series:

- RED'S MAGICK (SHORT STORY COLLECTION)
- SEEING RED (SHORT STORY)

Signs of the Prophecy Novels:

- YOUNGEST
- SEEKER
- CHOSEN (COMING SOON!)

Sorcha's Children Series:

- SORCHA'S CHILDREN (OMNIBUS EDITION)
- SORCHA'S HEART (NOVELLA)
- DRAGONS' CHOICE (NOVEL)
- DRAGONS' FLIGHT (NOVEL)
- DRAGONS' DESIRE (NOVEL)
- DRAGONS' DESTINY (NOVEL)

Supernatural Yellowstone Short Story Series:

- REALITY BITES
- THE CAT LADY OF YELLOWSTONE

Uncollected Anthology Short Stories:

- DEATH OF AN ALCHEMIST (UA ALCHEMY)
- THE WEDDING CAKE (UA MAGICAL ARTS)
- DARK OF THE MOON (UA PARANORMAL PIRATES)
- IN THE BANYAN COPSE (UA UNEXPECTED HISTORIES)
- OLD ONE (UA MAGICAL QUESTS)
- HAVE HOARD, WILL SEEK (UA A DIVERSITY OF DRAGONS)
- FLIGHT PLAN (UA MYSTICAL MAPS)
- DISAPPEARED! (UA WERE-CREATURES & CONUNDRUMS)
- MIDSUMMER NIGHT (UA SUMMER SOLSTICE)

Universal Star League Short Story Series:

- Voyages Into The Black (Collection)
- The Warbirds of Absaroka
- Awakening the Warrior
- Incident on the Odyssey
- The Queen's Captive
- The Lost Colony
- Freighter Families in Space

Witchling Short Story Series:

- Witchling
- The Solitary Sorceress
- To Protect a Princess

Stand Alone Novels:

- Second Sight

Historical Fiction:

- Her Highland Laird (Novella)
- Her Highland Yule
- Incident on the High Line
- Miss Bainbridge's Summer Adventure
- Miss Bainbridge's Christmas Party
- Sisters in Suffrage
- The Trail Where We Cried
- The White Dragon and the Red

Short Story Collections:

- A Flight of Dragons
- Love in a Flash
- Tales of Bygone Days
- Tales of Love & Magick
- Tales of the Unexpected
- Tales of Tomorrow

- TALES OF DISASTROUS DEEDS

Short Fiction:

- A GROVE OF MOUNTAIN ASH
- A WALK WITH GEORGIA
- AN ALIEN ADVENTURE
- ASTROMANCER
- BECAUSE OF THE CHRISTMAS STROLL
- BENEATH AND BEYOND
- DEEP DREAMING
- DELIA'S DECISION
- EGG THIEF
- ENCHANTMENT, INC.
- GOD-TOUCHED
- ICE STORM
- INCIDENT ON THE HIGH LINE
- IN SEARCH OF A VALENTINIAN
- IZZIE
- JOLLY WELL DONE
- KEYSTROKES & INTUITION
- MISS BAINBRIDGE'S CHRISTMAS PARTY
- MISS BAINBRIDGE'S SUMMER ADVENTURE
- NEEDLE-GREEN
- NEW YEAR
- OPENING HER EYES
- REMEMBRANCE
- SILVER-TIPPED DEATH
- SIMON SAYS
- SISTERS IN SUFFRAGE
- SKYE DREAMS
- SPINNING
- THE TIE THAT BINDS
- THE TRAIL WHERE WE CRIED
- THE WHITE DRAGON AND THE RED
- TO DREAM OF FLYING
- TREASURES

- TRIAL ON THE TRAIL
- WAKINYAN'S VALLEY

"WDM Presents" Anthologies:

- SPUN YARNS UNWOUND, VOL. 1
- SPUN YARNS UNWOUND: VOL. 2
- SPUN YARNS UNWOUND: VOL. 3
- SPUN YARNS UNWOUND: VOL. 4
- SPUN YARNS UNWOUND: VOL. 5
- TALES OF MYSTERY & MAYHEM
- 2016: A YEAR OF SHORT FICTION
- 2017: A YEAR OF SHORT FICTION
- WDM PRESENTS: SHORT FICTION FROM 2018
- WDM PRESENTS: SHORT FICTION FROM 2019
- WDM PRESENTS: SHORT FICTION FROM 2020
- WDM PRESENTS: SHORT FICTION FROM 2021

PREVIEW: DELECTABLE MOUNTAIN QUILTING

If you enjoyed these stories, you may want to read *Delectable Mountain Quilting*, a quilt themed cozy mystery. Here's a sample chapter.

Kristiana Lundrigan, Kristi to her friends and family, stared out the picture window beside her breakfast table. She adored the view, showing as it did the majestic Absaroka Range, including Mount Cowen, the highest peak visible from her Paradise Valley home. Scooping the last bite of scrambled eggs onto her fork, she concentrated on allowing the peace of the mountain scenery to soothe her soul. Today would be exciting, perhaps even nerve-wracking. She wanted to start it as calmly as possible.

Her small house sat on the eastern edge of Garnet Gateway, Montana, giving her an unimpeded view of the open valley as it approached the foothills of the 'Sorkees. Kristi had known it was the home she'd been searching for the moment she saw it. Single story, three bedrooms, and a nicely updated bathroom with an old fashioned claw footed tub. The view from the breakfast nook had been the cherry on top as far as Kristi was concerned.

She'd converted the east facing bedroom into a quilting studio, leaving the other two for a guest bedroom and her own use.

Designing her studio had been a delight. She'd finally had the space to create a floor-to-ceiling design wall by installing sheets of flannel-covered Homasote board on the largest unbroken wall. The flannel was the perfect touch. No need to pin her blocks to the wall (though the Homasote board was porous enough to allow for that if needed), they adhered to the flannel effortlessly.

Her sewing table, with its state-of-the-art Viking machine, sat in front of the room's only window, with the large cutting table on her left and the design wall to her right. Her ironing station stood behind her, near the closet, which had had its sliding doors removed and shelves built in to hold Kristi's fabric stash, stored quilts, and as-yet-unfinished projects. The final touch had been turning one of her early quilts into a Roman shade and hanging it over the entrance to the closet, protecting her stash of brightly colored fabric from too much light.

Kristi picked up her mug of mint tea from the scrubbed oak breakfast table and sipped the fragrant brew.

The divorce had been a painful blow, but it was in her past now. She was her own woman at last, with a home that suited her, and— in less than a week!— a business of her own. She was no longer Jason's wife, nor was she her father's little girl. She was

Kristiana Lundrigan, quilter, teacher, and soon-to-be business woman. An upstanding member of the Garnet Gateway community.

Garnet Gateway. She loved this small Montana town, nestled serenely in the Paradise Valley and guarded by the imposing Absaroka Mountains. She wasn't a native, hadn't been born in the town or even on one of the surrounding ranches, but Garnet Gateway was her home. Had been since she followed Jason here after her graduation from Montana State University in Bozeman. She'd been ready to follow him to Denver, where he'd worked his way up from patrol officer to homicide detective, but Jason had chosen to return home to Montana, to Garnet Gateway.

She'd married in Garnet Gateway. Established her first real home here, and had planned to grow old and die here. Still did, as a matter of fact. Only now she was alone.

Well, maybe not *exactly* alone.

As if summoned by her thought, Stitches and Between, her moggy cats, strolled into the kitchen and hopped lightly onto the window seat beside the table to join her. Stitches, the older of the pair, was a gray tabby female with four white paws. Between, named for the tiny, sharp needles used in hand quilting, was a little tuxedo male with the personality of a perennial kitten. Though Stitches was hardly a big cat, she outweighed Between by a good two pounds. The pair were best friends and excellent companions for Kristi.

"Well, good morning, you two," Kristi said, taking a moment to scratch behind first Stitches' ears and then Between's. "What have you been up to while I was eating?"

Stitches settled onto the cushioned window seat, front paws folded beneath her chest, purring contentedly, while Between nipped Kristi's finger gently... always ready to remind her that she was *his* human. He was happy to share her affection with Stitches, of course, but Between was a possessive little fellow.

Kristi nodded. "I love you too, Between." She understood possessive. And loyalty. And trust.

Jason, her ex-husband, had failed in all three areas. He'd had a brief affair during an out of town convention, and while he'd been honest enough to confess (when she confronted him with clear evidence), he'd failed to understand her possessiveness, or her expectation of loyalty, or that he'd forfeited her trust. He'd expected her to forgive and forget and for their lives to continue as if his indiscretion had never happened.

Unfortunately for him, Kristi wasn't built that way. She was too aware of her own worth to allow herself to be treated with such casual disrespect.

None of that changed the fact that she loved him.

Always had.

Always would.

But she'd divorced him anyway.

She refused to live with a man she couldn't trust, so despite a broken heart, she did what needed to be done and moved forward into a new, solitary life.

But when she closed her eyes…

…it was Jason's face that floated to the top of her consciousness.

He might not fit every woman's definition of handsome, but he had always been her gold standard. High forehead, strong jaw, steely gray eyes that could go all soft and almost blue when his emotions were high.

She tried to keep him out of her thoughts, and was mostly successful during the day… but nights were a different matter.

When she climbed into bed each night, usually with a cat curled on either side, she'd dream of Jason. Of running her fingers through his wavy chestnut hair, the thick mass of it like silk between her fingers. Or she'd giggle again as his unshaven chin scratched her cheek after a sensuous night of intimate pleasure.

And... Oh!... did she dream of the pleasures of making love to him!

Only to wake at dawn mourning the loss of the life they'd built together. The life she'd expected to continue until death parted them.

Busyness kept her going. She exorcised Jason from her days by constant activity. Meetings with the divorce attorney. Moving from the home they had shared into an apartment until their affairs (what an appropriate word!) were settled. Designing quilt patterns and then choosing fabrics and making sample blocks. Anything to keep herself from remembering that he had betrayed her. That he didn't love her... or at least didn't love her enough.

When the dust settled and the divorce was final, Kristi found that she had sufficient funds to buy a house in Garnet Gateway. She launched herself into the real estate market, determined to find the perfect home. She knew exactly what she wanted: a small house with enough space for a dedicated quilting studio; and when she found it, she didn't hesitate.

Not quite a year as a single woman and Kristi had taken back her maiden name, bought a home, and adopted Stitches and Between. She'd just begun to think about quitting her part-time secretarial job and establishing a career as a quilt artist when she'd learned that the local quilt shop was for sale.

Talk about perfect timing!

She'd made an appointment with her accountant, crunched some pretty amazing numbers, and determined that the inheritance her maternal grandmother had left her would be enough to not only make the down payment, but would allow for some remodeling if she planned carefully.

Nanna Van Oss would be pleased and proud to know she'd helped Kristi realize her dream of owning her own business, and a quilt shop was an apt use for the money. After all, Nanna was the one who'd taught Kristi to quilt.

Kristi had toured the quilt shop that very day, jotting down ideas for how she would use the space, as well as noting renovations that she'd want to see made. She'd made an offer that same afternoon, and then, praying for a quick acceptance, had begun to load her stitches, nice and even, so that when she pulled the needle through she wouldn't have to stop and pick any of them out.

She'd filled out the application for a small business loan, set up telephone interviews with several contractors, and used her notes to draw up plans for the renovations she hoped to make. With her plans in place, she'd settled back to wait for the current owner's response.

Mattie Stebbings, while not exactly a friend, was someone she knew on sight. Kristi often bought her quilting cottons from Mattie's shop and the women were both members of the statewide quilt guild. Kristi had hoped that Mattie would find her an acceptable beneficiary for the shop.

The wait hadn't been long. Less than twenty-four hours after the offer was made, Mattie accepted. Kristi's small business loan was also approved in short order, and the closing for the quilt shop was fast-tracked. In a mere thirty days, Kristi would own *Delectable Mountain Quilting*!

That was twenty-five days ago. Closing was now only five days away. Come Monday, the shop would be hers.

Time to meet with her chosen contractor and set the wheels in motion.

That was her agenda for today.

She'd arranged to meet Mark Robards, her contractor, at the shop this morning. Mattie, who seemed unusually anxious to consummate the sale, had closed the store as soon as she'd accepted Kristi's offer for the business, which included the building, land, and inventory, so the realtor, Stacy Akins, would also be present. Kristi intended to outline her desired changes and expected Mark to provide a detailed estimate of the cost.

Turning her gaze to the mountains once more, Kristi took a

deep breath, held it for a moment, then released it slowly. Everything was going to work out. She just knew it. Mark would give her a reasonable bid; the remainder of Nanna Van Oss's gift would more than cover the work; and the closing papers would be signed on Monday.

Each stitch in the last twenty-five days had followed the last, neat as a pin. These final steps would as well.

Glancing at the cats, she grinned. "It's going to be an exciting day, kids. You two will soon be quilt store cats!"

Look for *Delectable Mountain Quilting* at your favorite online retailer.

ABOUT DEBBIE MUMFORD

Debbie Mumford specializes in speculative fiction (fantasy, paranormal romance, and science fiction) as well as mystery and historical fiction. Author of the popular *Sorcha's Children* series, Debbie loves the unknown, whether it's the lure of space or earthbound mythology. Her work has been published in multiple volumes of *Fiction River*, as well as in *Heart's Kiss Magazine*, *Amazing Monster Tales*, and many other popular anthologies. She writes about dragon-shifters, time-traveling lovers, and detectives—whether amateur or professional—for adults as <u>Debbie Mumford</u>, and science fiction and fantasy for tweens and young adults as <u>Deb Logan</u>.

Join Debbie's special announcement newsletter list and receive a FREE story!

To learn more, visit Debbie at:
debbiemumford.com/
Or send her an email at:
deborah.mumford@gmail.com

facebook.com/DebbieMumfordWrites
amazon.com/author/debbiemumford
bookbub.com/authors/debbie-mumford
x.com/deborah_mumford